Hawk's Redemption

Stephanie Webb Dillon

Copyright © 2024 by Stephanie Webb Dillon

All rights reserved.

No part of this publication may be reproduced, distributed, or transmitted in any form or by any means, including photocopying, recording, or other electronic or mechanical methods, without the prior written permission of the publisher, except as permitted by U.S. copyright law. For permission requests, contact [include publisher/author contact info].

The story, all names, characters, and incidents portrayed in this production are fictitious. No identification with actual persons (living or deceased), places, buildings, and products is intended or should be inferred.

Book Cover Artist: Michelle RLS Sewell with RLS Imaging, Graphics and Designs.

Cover Model: Ryan Stanton

Photographer: Reggie Deanching with RplusM Photo

First edition 2024

SAMHSA'S (Substance Abuse and Mental Health Services Administration) National Helpline, 1-800-662-HELP (4357). (also known as the Treatment Referral Routing Service), or TTY: 1-800-487-4889 is a confidential, free 24-hour-a-day, 365-day a-year information service, in English and Spanish, for individuals and family members facing mental and/or substance use disorders. This service provides referrals to local treatment facilities, support groups, and community-based organizations.

Also visit the online treatment locator or send your zip code via text message: 435748 (HELP4U) to find help near you.

I have included this information as a way to hopefully reach out to those in need. My daughter is an addict, I pray for her every day that she will get help. She has lost many friends to suicide and overdose. If this helps anyone then it is worth it.

About the Author

Stephanie Webb Dillon resides in Memphis, Tennessee. She is married and has three daughters and six grandchildren. Stephanie enjoys spending time with her friends having game nights and crafting. Writing is her passion. She has completed her first book series this year and started two more. She is looking forward to traveling to book events in the next couple of years, meeting other authors, models, photographers and her readers.

You can follow her on her page at amazon.com/author/sdillon9614

Also By

Also, by Stephanie Webb Dillon

Freedom Colorado Series:
Baked with Love
Playing for Keeps
Sheriff's Convenient Bride
Daddy's Second Chance
The Scars Within
Guarding her Heart

Men of Phoenix Security Series:
Hidden Desires
Uncovering her Secrets

Rippers MC Series:
Undertaker's Match
Christmas Boyfriend
Hawk's Redemption

1

Hawk

Christmas at the clubhouse was always a bit rowdy. We had our big dinner with all the guys and their families, then a few hours later the single guys had a party. There would be a lot of alcohol, sweet butts and lots of sex all over the common area. We made sure there were bowls of condoms on several tables around the room. Nobody was looking for surprises. I have partaken in this many times and to be honest I could use the release right now. Bethann and the boys had been staying at my house most of this week. I moved them in after her sister was killed, leaving the boys orphans. We didn't know who their father was, just that he had never been in the picture. I wanted to know they were safe. Truthfully Bethann had been my fantasy for months. I worked security at our strip club 'Trixie's', being the son of one of the toughest meanest bastards in the Rippers' MC Chapter in Boston, was a learning experience I wouldn't wish on anyone. Seamus McKay was a mean bastard. My mother tried her best to keep me away from him but when I turned sixteen, he came calling. He took me to the clubhouse and introduced me to club life. I was set up to lose my virginity to several sweet butts. Pop got me drunk and put me in a room with them. They were all over me. I was immersed in that life for two years. When I graduated high school, I joined the marines. It was my ticket out of Boston, I served for twenty years then retired at thirty-eight. I had served with a few of the guys here and they suggested I ask about trying to work my way into the Rippers' here is Liberty. Since the Liberty chapter was the founding one, I only had to prospect and get patched in through them. I worked hard, did whatever was asked of me and patched in two years later. I have been a patched member for the last five years. I mostly work security at the strip club and do odd jobs on the side. We are legit and have several businesses that make money in the area. It wasn't always that way, but Undertaker changed things when he became president and it has continued under Axle.

I took over one of the houses on the compound from a member that had passed a couple years ago. I usually kept to myself. I enjoyed the benefits of being a single patched member, but I kept my sexual escapades to the clubhouse. I never brought any of the women to my house. I had participated in plenty of depravity over the last few years. I had never noticed or gave any woman the time of day outside of a quick fuck or a one-night stand. I noticed some of the club whores could get territorial and I wasn't dealing with that.

It was getting close to ten and I needed to get Bethann and the boys back to my place before the girls started to arrive. I didn't want them around that. Of course, Bethann knew what went on. She helped find women that were interested in servicing the club members. She never participated but plenty of the strippers did. I walked over to the couch and picked up Cameron. I left Joshua for Bethann since he was smaller. We had walked over since we were so close.

"Beth, can you grab Josh. We need to head out before it gets rowdy here." I said quietly as she looked up from talking to Annie and Sophie. She smiled when she saw Cameron sacked out over my shoulder. She got up and hugged the girls.

"Sure, we need to get them in bed, and I'm exhausted." Beth walked over and scooped up Josh walking towards the door. I jerked my head at the guys and followed her to my place. I left the door unlocked so we went on in and put the boys to bed. I had picked up a twin bed and a crib for the boys. We laid them down pulling off their socks and shoes. We changed them into their Christmas pajamas after dinner. Turning on their nightlight, I also clicked on the baby monitor and pulled the door closed.

"I'm going to take a bath and crawl into bed." Beth turned to go to the bathroom. I heard the water running and wondered if she was naked. I considered going back to the clubhouse for the party, but I just wasn't really interested. I went into the kitchen, got a beer and turned the tv on low to watch the football game I had recorded earlier. I could hear light splashing from her washing and I could not help but imagine her naked in that clawfoot tub. She had pale blonde hair long straight down to the top of her ass. Pale blue eyes like those you would see in a husky. Full pink lips and skin like porcelain. She was easily the most beautiful woman I had ever seen. I had been watching her for months, honestly, since she started working at Trixie's. First, I watched to see if she was going to be easy to manipulate. A lot of the dancers could be manipulated. I also had to watch Ritchie around her. He had been a real sleaze. She held herself above reproach. She was smart, efficient and fair. She didn't take any shit from anyone and so the girls were very respectful. She took care of them. Her sister Candy had started working at the club when she first came to town and then after she was cleared to work from having Josh. It was a damn shame what happened to her. We were still investigating that. I laid my head back on the recliner and closed my eyes for a few minutes.

I must have dozed off because I heard a gasp and a squeal as I looked up and saw Beth standing outside the bathroom in nothing but a towel. She was blushing and quickly ran to her room. I was still licking my lips thinking about the drops of water dripping from the strands of hair not fully put up down her lovely neck to her cleavage. Beth was a real woman, with full curves, large breasts and thighs made to cradle a man's hips. I wanted her under me so bad I could taste it. I turned the game off, poured out my beer and went to bed. I needed to get some rest.

2

Bethann

I laid in the tub soaking. Thinking about the past week and how crazy it had been. First my sister gets killed, outside of my job no less; then I am left to raise my two young nephews. Living in a studio apartment and working nights at a gentleman's club is not conducive to raising two small children. I have been working at Trixie's for almost two years now. I loved my job, but I knew I had to find something else. I planned to petition the court for guardianship of my nephews after the holidays. I called and asked what the requirements would be and the social worker told me I had to have a stable home with a separate bedroom for the boys and a job that allowed me to be available to them in the afternoons and evenings. I did not give my name, just asked general questions. The Rippers had been very good to me since I started working for them. They paid really well and always had security around to keep the customers in line. Hawk was their head of security for the club. He worked on the door most nights. He never crossed a line, but I could feel his gaze burn through me. Hawk was a walking wet dream. He was tall but not towering, with a very cut physique, tan like he worked outside a lot with piercing green eyes that seemed to see right through you. I have had many fantasies of him while using my vibrator. When he stepped in and took us to his place to live, I was shocked. He had a nice three-bedroom house on the compound. It had a nice open living area and two full bathrooms. It was made for a family. I was actually shocked to find out he lived here. The house was clean and sparse for furniture. I could tell he had furnished the boys' room right before coming to get us.

I drained the water and got out to dry off. Shoot I forgot to bring clothes in here. Well, Hawk had probably gone back to the clubhouse to get laid so I would just wrap a towel around me and sprint for my room. I opened the door and looked up in time to see Hawk glance up and pierce me with a smoldering look of hunger. I squealed and ran to my room, closing the door. I leaned against it for a minute, willing my heart to slow down. I wonder why he didn't go back to the party. Surely, he had needs. I placed the towel on a hook behind the door and got dressed in my pajamas. I sat on the end of the bed and braided my hair. If I left it loose for sleep it tangled. I really wanted to go get a glass of water, but I didn't want to face him again tonight. I laid down and grabbed my kindle off the nightstand. Maybe if I read for a little bit, I will be able to sleep.

I woke up to Cameron screaming, I jumped up and looked at the clock to see it was only four in the morning. I didn't want him to wake Hawk, so I ran next door to his room. I gently pushed open the door to find Hawk had already picked him up and was bouncing him on his big chest. Cameron had put his thumb in his mouth and just stared at the biker. He was still breathing heavily, but he was calming down. Of course, the screams woke up Josh; I reached in and rubbed his back making soothing noises until he fell back asleep. I sat up and watched Hawk with my nephew.

"Hey little man, you have a bad dream?" he asked in his gravelly voice. Cameron nodded his head still staring at the big man holding him. "I won't let anyone hurt you. You, your brother and your aunt are all safe with me. Okay buddy?"

"I's scared, I want my mommy." Cameron said in a quiet voice. They knew she wasn't coming back but sometimes when they had bad dreams they forgot. "Aunt Bethie, where is mommy?"

"Oh baby, Mommy went to heaven to live with the angels, remember?" I told him as a tear rolled down my cheek. "She didn't want to leave you or your brother, but she had to. She is always watching you both. She sends love to you."

"Aunt Bethie, you won't leave us, will you?" he asked in a soft voice, his eyes pleading with me.

"I will do whatever I have to do to stay with you and Josh forever. I promise. I love you both so much." Rubbing his back, I leaned over and kissed the top of his head. Hawk just looked at me with sympathy. "Why don't I lay down with you and help you go back to sleep?"

"Okay" he whispered rubbing his eyes. Hawk gently laid him back on his little bed and I laid down beside him. Rubbing his back like I did his brothers. I sang to him softly and waited for him to fall back to sleep. Hawk quietly left the room. The boys liked me to sing to them. Candy always did that, so it was comforting. I missed my sister so much. She was seven years younger than me and had been wild while I was the responsible one. She got mixed up with a man she said was bad and couldn't get away from him for a long time. When she was pregnant with Josh, he hit her so hard she fell onto a coffee table and almost lost the baby. She ran after that. She had been living in New York and wanted a fresh start. She refused to give me their father's name. They were not married so the boys had our last name. She wanted to keep it that way. I worried that maybe he found her and killed her. I was terrified the man would be coming for my nephews and I had no way of knowing who he was. I covered Cam up and got off the bed. I pulled the door closed figuring they would both sleep in this morning. I was exhausted but there was no way I was going back to sleep now.

I turned to walk toward the kitchen and saw Hawk standing there in nothing but his jeans making a pot of coffee. My mouth was so dry, and I just stood there staring at him. My panties were wet and getting uncomfortable. I had not been with a man in years. Hawk turned around and just stared at me with that hungry expression again. I realized I was just wearing a long t-shirt and panties. There was really no point running back to my room to change yet.

"Good morning" I mumbled reaching for a cup to fix myself some coffee. Hawk handed me a mug and poured me the first cup, pulling my favorite creamer from the fridge. He poured his black with touch a splash of cream and took a sip still perusing my body with his eyes.

"Would you like some toast? I was going to make breakfast, but I figure it will be a while before the boys get up. They had a late night." Hawk watched me closely. I guess he was always watching which is likely how he got his road name.

"No thanks, I don't like to eat this early." I told him as I stared at his chest. I mean if he was going to run around with no shirt then I wouldn't feel bad about enjoying the view. "I thought you would have gone back to the clubhouse to get your needs met last night. Bubbles couldn't talk about anything else for weeks last time."

"Oh, that was her name?" he said with a raised eyebrow. "I wasn't interested in anything being offered over there." Hawk stood up, took another drink of his coffee and headed towards the bathroom. "I'm gonna shower, I have some things to do around here."

I watched him go into the master bedroom and close the door. I let out the breath I didn't realize I was holding. I had a good thing here and I could not afford to fuck it up. Although I wasn't sure what the social worker would think about us being shacked up in a biker's house on their compound. At least I had my own room, and the boys had their room. I crossed my legs and continued to sip on my coffee. The newspaper was sitting on the table, so I opened it to the want ads. I really needed to find another job. I looked but couldn't find anything. I got up and put my cup in the sink and went to get dressed. It was cold so I put on some jeans and a sweater. I brushed out my hair and then pulled it back into a low ponytail and put on just a bare minimum of makeup. It was Sunday so there wasn't much I could do on the job search today. I came out of the room and started to make some pancakes. The boys loved them, they were cheap and easy. I had a huge stack made when Hawk came out of his room, wearing jeans and a long sleeve shirt that fit him just right. He filled out those jeans well too. Mercy, I shook my head and turned back to the stove.

"That sure smells good Beth." Hawk said as he walked behind me to pour himself more coffee. I could smell his aftershave and it was making my girl parts dance.

"There is plenty, fix yourself a plate. I thought I heard the boys so I'm going to go get them for breakfast." I glanced up at him and he smiled at me. I ran across the room to keep from doing what I really wanted to do. Opening the boy's door, they were sitting on the floor playing with their racetrack set that Hawk had bought them for Christmas. He had spoiled the boys. It was really sweet. I pulled my phone out of my back pocket and snapped a couple of pictures of them.

"Hey guys, pancakes are ready. Go wash your hands. Cameron help Joshie please?" I said as I turned and saw that Hawk had fixed them some milk in their cups. They also had their plates fixed. I looked up at him and smiled.

"Thanks, that's a big help." About that time Cameron came walking towards the table with Josh holding his hand. Hawk picked Josh up and put him in his high chair and Cameron climbed into the chair beside him. The boys had never really had a father figure in their lives. Their birth father was barely around long enough to knock up Candy and since she left when she was pregnant with Josh, he has never even seen him. Hawk is so good with the boys they just soak up all the attention he offers them like little sponges. Hawk fixed his plate and sat down beside me at the table. He was close enough that our legs touched, which of course had my body in overdrive. We finished our breakfast in silence listening to the boys' chatter about their toys from Santa. I blushed glancing over at Hawk who was smiling from ear to ear. He had enjoyed setting up Santa for them so much. It was really cute. I enjoyed watching him while he set up the racetrack and the train set.

We were about finished when Cameron knocked over his cup and it busted open all over the floor. I jumped up to clean up the mess and noticed that Cameron was staring at Hawk like he was afraid. I looked at him as I wiped up the spilt milk from the floor. He just plucked my nephew out of his chair and put him in his lap.

"It's ok Cam, accidents happen. I drop stuff all the time." He said gently to my nephew who visibly relaxed in his arms. If he didn't stop being so wonderful and understanding I was going to fall for him. I really needed to guard my heart better than that. I knew that while these were basically good guys, most of them behaved like man whores. I had heard the girls from the club talk, and I knew that Hawk was a favorite among them. They tried hard to get him more than once. I had heard stories of his prowess in bed. Seeing him day in and day out had piqued my curiosity for sure, but I couldn't afford to make a mistake. I had two kids to raise, and I had to find a job. I wet a washcloth and cleaned the boys up then sent them to sit in the floor in front of the tv to watch cartoons while I cleaned up the breakfast dishes.

"What are your plans for the day?" I asked him as I sat down with another cup of coffee. "I have to find a job. I can't stay here forever."

"You can stay as long as you like, and I may have a lead on a job for you." Hawk said as he put his jacket on and grabbed his keys. He looked at the boys for a minute and back at me. He smiled and I swore I was going to have to change my damn panties. "I'll be back in a few hours. Just relax and spend time with your nephews."

He left and I was standing there with my jaw hanging open. Cam came over and tugged on my shirt. I looked down and he was smiling at me. I scooped him up and carried him over to the couch sitting down with him in my lap. If Hawk says he may have found me a job, then I would just trust him and enjoy my time with my nephews.

3

Hawk

I knew that Gears and Sophie went back to work the day after New Years and that they had to fire their receptionist at the firm. I figured Bethann was plenty qualified for that position and while it may not pay as much, she doesn't have to worry about paying rent anymore. I was going to do my best to convince them that they could stay with me as long as she wanted. I really liked her, I just needed to figure out how to get that across without running her off. I pulled up to Gears' home and went to knock on the door. I heard peals of laughter coming from inside and wondered if I was interrupting. I was just about to go to my car and call when the front door opened, and Gears stood there with whipped cream and sprinkles on his face. I just stood there a moment and blinked. Then I burst out laughing.

"What the hell happened to you man?" I asked my wiping my eyes. He grabbed the damp cloth that Sophie handed him and proceeded to wipe his face off and he ushered me inside.

"Rogue pancake." Was all he said as he went toward the bathroom. "Be right out." He swatted Sophie's ass as he passed her, and I could see she was struggling not to laugh some more.

"Good morning, Hawk, how was your Christmas?" she asked me as she went to pour me a cup of coffee. I took it from her and smiled.

"Thanks sweetie. It was nice, the boys had a great time, and they are loving their toys." I told her as I took a sip of my coffee.

"How is Bethann?" she asked with a concerned expression. "I can't imagine losing Pammy and we don't even get along most days."

"She is trying to stay focused on the boys. I don't think she has really given herself a chance to grieve yet. The state will eventually want to do check-in's and look into her ability to care for Cameron and Joshua. They are the only family she has left, and she is terrified of losing them. That's actually one of the reasons I'm here this morning."

Gears walked back into the living room with fresh clothes on and walked up behind Sophie wrapping his arms around her waist. He looked at me for a minute as he took a sip of his own coffee and then nodded.

"I called Lee this morning and told him that I had our front desk situation handled. I know Bethann. She is meticulous, hardworking and great with people. She would be a welcome addition to H&W Accounting." Gears loaded the dishes in the dishwasher and started it before sitting down and pulling Sophie into his lap. "I had planned to come by today to talk to her and offer her the job. We would pay her more than we paid Brittni, simply because she has more experience and can take on more duties." He held Sophie close. I knew it was sore subject since the woman had kidnapped and shot his woman last week. She was still recovering from a gunshot wound in her shoulder.

"That sounds great. Please make sure she knows it was your idea not mine. I am already struggling getting her to accept a home with me."

I ran my hand over my face in frustration. "I want to get to know her better, but I don't want to push too fast. Her life has been upended by all the drama with Candy's death."

"Maybe we could keep the boys for a few hours so you two can have time alone or so that she can just let go and cry." Sophie suggested softly. "I love kids and I need practice before my niece or nephew arrives."

"That would be great." Getting up from the table I put my cup in the sink. "I need to get going I want to swing by the club and look around the back. See if there is anything that the cops missed. I also need to make some calls and I didn't want Bethann to overhear me."

"Do you need any help?" Gears asked as Sophie got up to go get dressed for the day. "I know you're looking into who the boys' father could be."

"I'll let you know; I have some guys from Phoenix looking into it." I told him, putting my jacket back on. "I'll probably have one of them following her until we find out what the connection is. They still don't know who killed Candy."

"I don't mind extra security hanging around, it will keep Sophie safer as well." Gears said glancing towards the bedroom where Sophie went to get ready for the day. "We will head over to your place shortly to talk to Bethann about the job. She would be doing us a huge favor."

"Thanks, I'm going to head out. I have some things I need to do for the club, and I want to see if anyone has been hanging around that looks out of place. I had Phoenix put in a new security system at the club after Candy was killed. I can pull the feed up at home, but I'd rather not have Bethann see something she shouldn't." I waved and headed out.

Gator waved at me as I pulled up to the gate. I gave him a nod and took off towards town. The club was on the edge of town, pulling up to the back I parked and got out to look around. I went inside and started a pot of coffee in the office before firing up the computer. The boys looked nothing like their mother or their aunt. Both were blondes with blue eyes. The boys had dark hair and a darker complexion with brown eyes. I poured myself some coffee and sat down to go through the security feed for the past week. Fang had been keeping the place going since Bethann had quit. Reviewing video could be very boring and sometimes didn't produce anything, but I had a feeling that whoever killed Candy would be snooping for the kids. They likely knew that Bethann was their aunt. I didn't want anyone bothering her or the boys. I heard a noise and then Fury popped his head in the door.

"Hey man, I figured I would find you here since you weren't at home. I got something you may find interesting." Fury said as he sank his large frame down on the couch in the office. "I noticed some guys driving by the club pretty regularly the last couple of days. I've been watching that security feed for the outside. Looks like the Italians."

"Mafia?" I said as I pulled up the feed for the outside cameras. Sure enough, the same Cadillac kept coming by in the evening. It would be parked across from the club and sit there for hours. Someone was staking out the place. The back window rolled down and I got a glimpse of the passenger. "Well, I'll be damned if that isn't Enzo Sartori. Italian scum."

"You thinkin' what I am?" Fury asked as he glanced at the screen again. I knew what he was getting at because it was running through my head too. "Those boys have a strong Italian look to them. Candy was very secretive about their paternity. She never spoke of a boyfriend or a father. Could be she got mixed up with someone she shouldn't have."

"If those boys are Italian mafia royalty, we are going to have a problem." I cursed under my breath. "Thing is, I'm not sure how much

Bethann knows about their father. I'm going to have to have a talk with her about that later. Make sure you are helping at the club this week. I want to know if they come back during working hours. Who they talk to and what questions are asked?" I closed the computer and got up to leave. I wanted to get back to the house and talk to Bethann while the boys were down for their nap. "Call me when you hear something."

"Will do Hawk." Fury said before he locked up and took off. I watched him drive back towards the clubhouse. He seemed to be spending a lot of his time around home lately. Lillian was there a lot as well, maybe that was a good thing.

4

Bethann

I was doing some laundry when I heard a knock on the door. I was startled at first but there wouldn't be strangers here on the compound. I glanced over to see the boys playing with their cars, half watching one of their programs. I walked to the door and checked the peephole to see Gears and Sophie standing there. I opened the door and stepped back to let them inside.

"Hey guys, what's up?" I asked as they came in. Sophie went to sit down and play with the boys. Gears nodded to the kitchen table, and I followed him over and sat down. "Can I get you anything to drink?"

"We're fine. We just finished breakfast. I heard you were looking for a job." Gears said smiling over at Sophie and the boys. They were such a sweet couple. I was very happy for him. I looked back at him, and I knew I looked embarrassed and surprised. "I know that due to the change in your circumstances that you needed to make some changes in your life. I think I can help with that."

"Now look, I don't want some charity job that you made up. I know ya'll want to help take care of us. I appreciate that but I can take care of my nephews." I said with my head held up.

"Bethann, I have been around you for years. I have seen how you manage the club and the employees. You are smart and a hard worker. We had to fire our secretary right before Christmas. I'm sure you may have heard about what happened to Sophie." He said looking over at his girl. She gave him a soft smile and picked Joshua up to sit in her lap. Cameron had brought her a book to read. "I know that you would be an asset to us at the firm. We need the help, and I would much rather hire someone that I can trust."

"Oh, well what about the boys. I need to find childcare for them. I can't afford to pay for the daycare that Candy had them in. I don't know how she paid for it." I was running ideas through my head when Hawk came in the door. I smiled at him, and he winked at me. "Hawk, they offered me a job."

"We were just about to go through the benefits. She was concerned about paying for the boys' daycare." Gears said raising his eyebrows at Hawk. I wondered what that was about. "So first you will start at forty thousand a year with a raise after your first ninety days. Full benefits for you and the boys along with paid holidays and twenty-one days of paid leave. Monday through Friday from nine to five with half an hour paid lunch break."

"That's very generous of you. I would love to accept. I'll manage childcare." I said watching the boys curled up to Sophie asleep. They were my priority now and this was a chance to give them the future they deserved.

"I have an idea about childcare if you are interested, I'll need to make a call first then we can talk about it." Hawk said pulling his phone out of his pocket and shooting off a text to someone, his phone beeped with a response, and he chuckled. "Bethann, you know Lillian, right?"

"Well yes, she is a nice lady, but what does she have to do with my childcare dilemma?" I asked as I got up to fix some coffee. The doorbell rang and I cringed glancing to see if it woke the boys up. Thankfully they were still out. Hawk went to open the door and he stepped back to allow Lillian to come in.

"Hi Bethann. I thought it would be better if I came over and talked to you myself. I hope that's okay." Lillian said as she came over and took a seat at the table. "I know we don't know each other well but I have been around these guys a long time. I was pregnant when my old man was killed. I ended up losing my baby and couldn't bring myself to go back to work at the daycare center after it happened. It was too hard being around all the babies knowing mine was gone. I am in a much better place now, but they don't have any openings in town. I'd love to take care of the boys while you work. We could work out an affordable payment for me that doesn't put you in a bind and gives me a little bit of spending money. It also allows them to stay here where it's safe."

I sat and found myself smiling. That makes me feel so much better. I don't know who the boys' father is and I was worried about him getting to them if that's why Candy ended up dead. This way they would be protected. I got up and gave her a hug. I was so relieved to have a job. I mean I loved being here with Hawk and I wasn't in any hurry to leave but at least now I would eventually have options. I glanced up and he was watching me. It felt like he was always watching. It made me hot the way he looked at me. He shook his head and went to pick up Cam and take him to his room, a few minutes later he came and took Josh from Sophie and put him in his crib. Gears looked at him and then smiled.

"We don't start back to work until the day after New Years so you have a week to let the boys get used to Lillian and you can fill out your insurance paperwork early so I can get it filed as soon as we open back up. The dress code is business casual. Your wardrobe for the club is fine. If you have any questions, you have my number. Oh yeah, at work call me Austin or Mr. Wilson. The other employees don't know I am a partner, so you need to remember I'm a coworker."

"Sure thing, Mr. Wilson." I said winking at him. Hawk growled and Sophie giggled. "Thank you so much. I will see you first thing a week from today." I glanced over at Hawk blushing. Gears chuckled and helped Sophie into her jacket as they left.

"We need to talk about your sister." He said as he took my hand and led me to the couch. "I hate to do this today when you have had such good news, but it's important."

"Of course, if it involves the boys, I'll do whatever I can to help." I told him as I sat beside him. Hawk looked at me for a minute and took my hand holding it. He looked like he was trying to figure out what to ask me. "You're making me nervous."

"I'm sorry babe, it's just I don't want to scare you. We have been watching the cameras around the club and Enzo Sartori has been spotted stalking the club. We were wondering if Candy could have been involved with him when she was in New York." He watched my face for my reaction. I wondered if the boys had some Italian heritage by their looks because their mother was blonde like me with pale skin and freckles. The boys have dark hair, brown eyes and a beautiful olive complexion. If I had not been there for the birth of Joshua, I would have doubted they could be hers.

"I'm not sure, she talked about a guy she was with in New York, but she would never tell me anything about what he did or give me his name. She would go weeks without calling and then I'd hear from her. She acted like nothing was wrong, but I didn't have her address. I thought it was weird." I told him this thinking back to that time wondering if there was anything I missed telling him. "I'm pretty sure she told me she was living in Brooklyn at one time. I just know one day she showed up at my apartment with Cameron in her arms. She asked if I could help her find a job. I got her on at Trixie's as a dancer because she didn't finish school and she needed a good income. I realized several months later that she was pregnant. I took her off the stage and had her waiting tables instead until after Joshua was born. She had money. I think she brought it with her but was afraid to use it until she had an income so she could justify spending any."

"I wonder if she took the money from him. It would make sense that he would come after her for it. Also knowing he had a kid might make him look for her. I'm surprised it took him this long to find her though. The Sartori family has a lot of money and connections. Makes me think maybe he knew where she was and kept waiting to see if she led him to the money. I guess he finally got impatient." Hawk said as he rubbed his fingers over my hand. I shuddered thinking about those people getting their hands on my nephews. "We need to go back to her apartment and do a thorough search of the place. You said she was paid through the end of the month. I'll send the guys to search the place, and I'll have Gears check her financials."

I realized that Hawk had stopped talking because I was staring at his mouth. I had wondered for months what it would feel like to be kissed by this man and he was sitting right beside me holding my hand. Suddenly his other hand was around the back of my neck and his lips covered mine. I wrapped my arms around his neck and climbed into his lap. He slid his tongue inside my mouth and mated with my own. It was a kiss of exploration and full of passion. He in turn licked and nipped at my bottom lip as we explored each other. When I heard the squeak of a door, I jumped off his lap.

Cameron was standing at his door rubbing his eyes. I walked over and picked him up, taking him to the kitchen to get him a drink. After getting him settled into a chair with some milk I turned to go get Josh when Hawk slid an arm around my waist and pulled me close for a minute.

"We will pick that back up later." he said as he kissed my nose and went out the door. All my girl parts were tingly, and I couldn't wait to find out what that would be like. Blushing I went back to fixing lunch for my nephews.

5

Hawk

I had to get out of there to settle down. I was hard as a rock and wanted nothing more than to throw her over my shoulder and take her to my bed. She has two toddlers that kept me from doing that during the day. I knew there was chemistry between us. I felt it any time we were in the same room, but I had not expected that instant combustion when I kissed her. She went off like sparks in my arms and I wanted more of it. I walked over to the clubhouse to see who was around.

Walking in the door I spotted Axle talking to Fury and Gears. They looked up and waved me over. Sitting on the sofa I nodded at Lillian who was bustling in the kitchen.

"I looked at Candy's financials and I am not finding anything out of the ordinary except that I don't see where she paid her rent using her account and there are no large cash withdrawals. I suspect she may have paid cash to the landlord. Question is, did she use her tips, or did she use money she has stashed." Gears said looking at his laptop in front of him.

"I have the keys to her place. How about if we head over do a search to see what we can find. If she is paying cash, she may not have given her real name and that may be why they found her at the club and not her place." I suggested to them. "She managed to stay under the radar for almost two years."

"Okay guys, now would be as good a time as any." Axle said as we all headed out the door. Thankfully when they grabbed Candy, she was between sets, so her personal items were all in her locker. I had the key to the apartment on my keyring. We kept an eye out for the Sartori's while we headed to her place. If we saw them, we would circle around and come back later. I had Gears with me and Axle rode with Fury. Pulling up at her building we looked around but didn't see anything out of the ordinary. As I walked into her apartment, I noticed that she had made it cozy and inviting. I had not paid it much attention when we grabbed the boys' things last week. She had tried to make a home for them here. We started searching through drawers, under the bed, the mattress and in the closets. I was back in the master bedroom when I noticed an old hat box in the corner of the floor. It was under a couple of shoe boxes. I picked it up and carried it to the bedroom. When I opened it at first, I thought it was just a hat box, but I noticed some green under the white tissue paper. Pulling out the hat and tissue paper I saw several large wads of cash. Damn looks like she stole a stash from the man's safe. That's probably why he didn't notice it immediately. I had a stash that I kept for emergencies too, but I kept mine locked in a safe. I looked around for something else to put the cash in.

"Hey guys, I'm in the master can one of you look and see if there is a paper bag or gallon size bag in the kitchen?" I said as I walked to the living room holding the box. Fury walked over and looked inside letting out a whistle.

"Damn, that's a lot of cash. This must be what gave her the means to leave him." Fury said as he reached inside and started to count the money. A couple of the bundles were opened so she must have just been taking what they needed to survive. "She was not living above her means, and she didn't spend extravagantly so there were no red flags. I wonder how they found her."

"I have some searches in the works and the guys at Phoenix are helping me get more background on her life in New York. I'm sure Stone will have something for me in a few days." Gears said as he handed me a brown lunch bag to stuff the money in. I wanted to put it in my jacket, so it wasn't obvious.

"Ok, do me a favor and send a prospect over to pack all of her things. I want her stuff moved to my storage room in my garage." I told them as I sent Bethann a text, checking on her and the boys. She responded back that they were fine, and dinner would be ready in about an hour. "Let's head back, I need to drop Gears off at his place and get home."

"You going to be working the door at the club this week?" Axle asked me. "I know you are very hands on with it. Maybe you will spot something someone else wouldn't."

"Yeah, I'll be there the next couple of nights." I told him as I climbed in my truck to leave. We headed back to the compound where I dropped Gears off at his place and headed to mine. I pulled up in time to see Lillian walking across to her place with a bag on her shoulder and a boy holding each hand talking nonstop to her. I waved and Cameron came running over to me.

"Mr. Hawk, we gonna have a sleepover with Ms. Lily." Cameron was so excited he was bouncing in place. "We gets to have pizza for dinner and watch a movie."

"That sounds like fun. You are both going to be good boys for her right?" I said in a firm voice. He nodded and ran back to take her hand.

She winked at me and jerked her head to the house. Well, this was an interesting turn of events. I would have Bethann to myself tonight. "Thanks Lillian, see you boys tomorrow."

Smiling, I whistled as I walked to my house. Finally, some alone time with my girl, well I hoped she would be my girl eventually. I let myself in and locked the door back. There was some music playing but I didn't see Bethann anywhere. I heard water running and realized she was taking a shower. I hung up my coat and kicked off my boots. It felt a little chilly in the house, so I started a fire. A few minutes later I heard singing and then she turned the corner wearing nothing but a towel. Her blonde hair was piled on top of her head, and she had drops of water dripping down her neck between her breasts. Her eyes widened when she saw me, and she took a step back against the wall. I walked up and pressed her between my body and the wall leaning down to kiss the water from her skin. She shivered and slipped a hand behind my head holding me to her. I looked at her and took hold of the towel when she didn't resist, I yanked it off of her. Stepping back to take her in I looked my fill. She was beautiful, all softness and curves. She started to cover herself and I shook my head. I started to kiss her neck, licking and biting her skin as I worked my way down to her ample breasts. As I suckled them, I ran one hand down her side then I knelt down to where I wanted to be. Slipping my hands around to her ass I pulled her close so I could smell her arousal. I leaned in for taste and groaned as her tart sweetness coated my tongue. Using my hands, I spread her legs a little more so that I could get to her. I explored her body with my fingers and tongue, loving her little whimpers and moans. When I felt her legs start to give, I stood and picked her up to carry her to my bed. I was nowhere near done feasting on her. Laying her back on my bed I took in the view again. She was stunning. All peaches and cream complexion with a few little freckles here and there on her body. She squirmed and started to cover herself again.

"Don't, I want to look at you. I have fantasized about this since the first time I saw you." I said as I reached up to kiss her. "You are better than anything I could have imagined."

"But I'm not in shape like the dancers that are always coming on to you. I don't really work out and I like food." She said blushing. Clearly Beth never saw the looks she got from men at the club. It's true she didn't flaunt her body and she wasn't a small woman, but she was built like the Hollywood actresses back in the Marilyn days and I loved it.

"You are gorgeous, now lay back and let me show you how much I like your body." I told her as I slid my finger into her tight wet channel and found her g-spot. I leaned back down and started to flick her clit with my tongue while I wiggled my fingers on the inside until she came hard screaming and gushing. It was the hottest thing I had ever seen. I watched her as I took off my clothes and got a condom out of my nightstand. I looked back at her as I rolled it on to see her licking her lips and staring at my chest. I did work out quite a bit and I knew I was cut. She obviously liked what she saw. I raised her legs up and lined myself up with her core before I entwined my hands with hers above her head and plunged into her warm body. She let out a loud cry and then her body started to spasm around me. It was all I could do not to spend like a teenager with just a few strokes. I held still a minute to get control of myself before I started working my cock in and out of her in a rhythm that worked for us both. I released her hands and then flipped us, so she was riding me. I wanted to watch her take her pleasure. Her eyes widened because this position had me deeper and I wasn't a small man. She bit her lip and put her hands on my pecs as she started to ride me, making swivels with her hips as she slid up and down my cock. I gripped her hips and helped her pick up speed and then suddenly she threw her head back and cried my name out while she came. I followed her and found my release as well. She laid her body over mine and tried to catch her breath.

"Wow, that was amazing. Can we do it again?" she asked with a giggle. I looked at her and smiled. Her stomach let out a growl and I chuckled. "Yeah, maybe after dinner."

We got cleaned up and she threw on my shirt while I grabbed a pair of joggers to throw on while we ate.

6

Bethann

We were sitting curled up on the sofa after having finished dinner. I had baked pork chops in a gravy, made mashed potatoes, green beans and some rolls. It was warming in the oven, so we didn't have to reheat anything. I was curled up against his chest and we were wrapped in a blanket watching some home improvement show. I was still blissed out from the best sexual experience of my life. Hawk was a very attentive lover.

"You know, it just occurred to me that I don't know your real name." I said glancing up at him. He smiled as he ran his hand up and down my back.

"Sean Patrick McKay, but I have been Hawk for a long time." He said as he kissed my head. "You can call me Sean if you like but only at home."

"Sean Patrick, good Irish name." I smiled at him as he tickled me. "I wondered with those pretty green eyes." He was a good man, a bit rough around the edges and dangerous for sure. Still, I knew I was safe with him. "Let's go to bed." I stood up and reached for his hand. His eyes were hot and hungry. I was ready for round two for sure. I pulled off his shirt as we entered the bedroom and dropped it on a chair, then I crawled onto the bed and turned to him as he walked over. "Take those off." I pointed to his joggers.

"How do you ask?" he said with a glint in his eye. I smirked and reached out to him with my hands on his waist. Looking up at him, I licked my lips and said "Please."

With a grunt he jerked them down and tossed them aside, stepping closer he wrapped his hand in my hair and held my head where he wanted it. I stuck my tongue out to lick the pre-cum from his crown before he pushed into my mouth. He wasn't too long but definitely girthy. I struggled to get my mouth around him, but it was worth the effort. As I licked and sucked him holding onto his hips for balance he moaned and caressed my face. He let me get a good feel for what I was doing before he backed away from me.

"I don't want to come in your mouth this time. Turn around and crawl up the bed a little." He instructed firmly. He followed behind me, grabbed onto my hips and rubbed his fingers up and down my slit. I was drenched. He used my own moisture and pushed a finger in me then two. Making sure I was ready before he plunged himself all the way inside me in one stroke. I came pulsing around him and he gave several thrusts before he was right there with me. Grabbing some tissues from beside the bed he cleaned us up and pulled me into his arms.

"Damn baby, you make me feel like a teenager again. I swear I have more stamina than that." He laughed as he ran his fingers through my hair. I giggled and ran my hand down his chiseled abs. I couldn't believe this beautiful man wanted me. "I have to work the club the next couple of nights. I'll go in around seven and work until close so it will be a couple of late nights. The guys are taking turns. I want you to promise me you will stay on the compound and keep your phone with you and charged at all times. Nobody should be able to get on the property that shouldn't be here but just the same check the peephole before you open the door to anyone and if you don't know them don't open the door and call me."

"Has there been trouble?" I asked him worried about the other employees. I had been manager for a while, so I knew everyone pretty well. "Is there anything I can do to help?"

"No trouble babe, we just don't want to hire anyone officially yet. We want to be able to ensure whoever we bring in will be legit." He rubbed my back to comfort me. "I just want you three to be safe. We haven't found who killed your sister yet and don't know the reason behind it. We have a few ideas but nothing concrete yet."

My mind was spinning with the possibilities. I knew he suspected the Italian mafia in New York. Candy had lived there for a few years, and I know she was living with someone while she was there. Hawk had seen one of the family here in town. It made my head hurt just thinking about what she had been involved in.

"Okay, we will be extra cautious. I'm glad the boys won't have to leave the property for daycare." I told him as I turned over onto my side. He turned out the lamp and then spooned me from behind. "Thank you for being here for us."

"Listen, I am here because I want to be. I want you and the boys in my life, and I will do everything I can to make sure you are safe and happy. Now sleep baby." He said as he kissed my head and pulled me close. I didn't think I would be able to sleep, but between the orgasms and the heat from the man behind me I found myself drifting off.

7

Hawk

Holding this woman is the best feeling ever. I laid awake until I felt her drift off to sleep. I let myself fall shortly after. Waking up beside her was even better. She had turned over at some point and draped herself across my body using my chest for a pillow. Her platinum blonde hair splayed over me like a silk curtain. I glanced over at the clock and saw it was about a quarter until eight. We needed to get up and shower before Lillian brought the kids back. I slid my hands under her arms and gently pulled her up my body so I could kiss her.

"Good morning baby." I whispered in her ear. She rubbed her face against my chest and then jerked her head back. Her eyes wide and then she relaxed. "You forget whose bed you were in baby?"

"Yeah, for a minute. I need to go to the bathroom." She said as she slid off the bed. I gave her a few minutes to take care of her needs before going into the bathroom and starting the shower for us both. She looked surprised as she was washing her hands and brushing her teeth.

"I figured we could take a shower together if that's okay with you." I asked her with a smirk. She was staring at my body, and I had morning wood. Frankly I stayed semi-hard around her most of the time anyway. "See something you like?"

She looked back up at me and smiled as she stalked over past me and got into the shower. I took care of my morning needs and then got in with her. She was wetting her hair, and I took the shampoo, poured some in my hands and started to lather it in her hair, massaging her scalp and making sure to get the ends. Turning her back toward the spray, she rinsed the shampoo out while I took the conditioner and repeated the process. Beth took the bodywash and poured some on a washcloth that she started using to wash my body. I watched her while she washed me, and she made sure she didn't miss any part of me. Next it was my turn and I made sure to soap her liberally using my hands to clean her up. She turned around so I could wash her back and then she put her hands on the tile and arched her back. I groaned and soaped my cock then grabbed her hips and pushed inside her. She moaned my name loudly. She continued to move back toward me and moan as I fucked her hard. I pulled out and turned her around picking her up I slid back inside and fucked her up against the wall. She had her arms wrapped around my neck and her head leaned forward into me. I leaned over and bit her on the shoulder and she started coming, legs trembling, and I went over with her. I had a bench in my shower, so I eased her down to sit on it while I cleaned her up with the shower head.

I got out and dried off then got another towel and dried her off. She smiled at me, still looking sleepy and very content. She started to run a comb through her hair and blow it dry. I got dressed and went to start some coffee for us. Checking my phone, I saw that Lillian planned to feed the boys lunch before bringing them back over. I looked up to see

Bethann coming into the living room in some jeans and a hoodie with her hair in two braids. She looked adorable.

"I made coffee, sit down and have some while I fix us some breakfast." I told her as I pulled out the eggs and bacon. I knew she wasn't used to having anyone do stuff for her, so I enjoyed it all the more. She smiled and fixed us both a cup knowing I liked mine black with a splash of cream. She added a little of her flavored creamer to hers as well. She pulled me to her for a kiss.

"Thank you, don't we need to go get the boys?" she asked me. "I don't want to take advantage of Lillian's kindness."

"She texted me that they boys were about to go down for their morning nap and she would bring them home after lunch." I told her as I put some bacon, eggs and toast in front of her. "Let's have breakfast. I have a few more things we should talk about before I have to go to work later."

"So, we found the money stash your sister had. It was evident that she only dipped into it when it was necessary. We have the money stashed in the clubhouse safe for now. I just wanted you to know that this could be what they were looking for." I watched for her reaction, and she seemed to come to some conclusion.

"I always wondered where the extra money came from. I mean she was very popular at the club, and she made great tips, but she never had trouble paying for the boys' daycare situation." She looked up at me and looked worried. "What if they try to get it from me?"

"Okay first baby, you need to remember that you will be working with Gears. He may not look like it, but he can be lethal. Second, you will have extra eyes on you at all times when you are not with me. We are not going to let those people get close enough to have a conversation with you much less hurt you. There is also a reason we have Lillian keeping the boys here on the compound. No one gets in here that we don't invite or screen through the gate. They are safer here than anywhere else and since they are not school aged yet, their names are not in the system. Candy had Doc administer all of their booster shots and he checked on them when they were sick." I plucked her out of the chair she was in and put her in my lap.

"What about the nights you work?" she asked looking nervous. "I know you say we are safe but what if someone manages to get past the gate?"

"I have a panic room; you enter it from the back of the pantry. It goes down into a basement. You can't tell it's there from the outside. I will program it to accept your handprint along with mine. If anything, weird happens, or you feel unsafe, take the boys and your phone and go down there. I have batteries and lights. It looks like a little apartment. There is a queen-size bed, a bathroom and a fridge. I keep nonperishable snacks down there. It is also soundproof, which is good since the boys would have a hard time being quiet." I set her off of my lap and took her hand leading her into the pantry. I programmed her print and then had her test it. I walked her downstairs and showed her the room suggesting we put a few of their toys down here. She nodded and followed me back upstairs and we went into the living room.

8

Bethann

My mind was spinning with all the information he had laid on me. I'm glad that he is straight with me though. I don't like to be kept in the dark. I have to know what I'm dealing with. He led me over to the couch and pulled up the internet on his laptop. He showed me pictures of the guys he thought were responsible. I had to admit the boys looked like one of them.

"You needed to see what these people look like, at least the ones we know of so if they try to come into the office you will know to alert Gears that they are there immediately. He can let the guys outside know in case they didn't get a good look at them." Hawk put his arms around me and pulled me close. "I swear I won't let anything happen to you or those boys."

"I know you won't, I trust you and the boys do as well." I mumbled against his chest, soaking in the comfort of his arms around me. We sat cuddled on the couch until Lillian showed up to drop off Cameron and Joshua. I could hear them chattering before she knocked. Hawk smirked and went to get the door. The boys ran straight to me. I hugged them both and got them settled with some toys on the floor. Lillian sat down in one of the armchairs beside the couch.

"I hope they weren't too much trouble." Hawk said as he put his arm around me. He watched the boys playing on the floor in front of us.

"They were a joy to have. No problems at all. I'm sure we will get on just fine." Lillian said smiling at us. "You just let me know what time you need to leave for work, and I'll be sure to be here ten minutes before that."

"Let me know if there is anything you need for next week. I'll be sure to pick it up." Hawk said. "We want you to be comfortable here while you keep them."

"Let me know what their favorites are, or if there are things they don't like." Lillian suggested. "It's easier if I don't try to feed them something that they don't like."

"They are pretty easy to please with food. Josh hasn't tried as much since he has just started eating solid foods in the last month. No allergies so far." I told her, trying to think of anything else she would need to know. "Cam has nightmares sometimes. Mostly in the evening but a couple of times during naps."

"Thanks for letting me know, I'll be sure to listen for him during naptimes." Lillian got up and put her purse on her shoulder. "I should head home; I have some cleaning to do. I'll talk to you this weekend."

"Bye Ms. Lily." Cameron yelled as Lillian went out the door. Hawk laughed at him as he ran to the door to hug her. I knew he was as happy as I was that the boys liked her. I hated that my sister wasn't going to get to see them grow up. Josh's little personality was growing every day, and he was such a sweet baby. I went to the door to lock it after Lillian left. Cameron looked out of the window as she walked to her house.

When he couldn't see her anymore, he walked over to the couch and climbed up into Hawk's lap.

Hawk sat on the floor and played with the boys for a while and I got things started for dinner. I had a few days left before I started my new job and I wanted to keep things as normal as possible for my nephews. Thankfully they were young and resilient.

Later that evening we sat at the table talking. The boys had been fed and put down. We were lingering over some coffee.

"Do you have everything you need to start work in a couple days?" Hawk asked me. "We could make a trip out shopping if needed."

"I'm good for now. Austin said my wardrobe for the club was fine for the office. None of my work clothes were inappropriate. Mostly slacks and knee-length skirts with nice blouses. My heels were not as high as what the dancers wore. I should be fine." I said blushing as his eyes got hot while I was talking about my heels. I knew he liked my legs. I had noticed him staring on several occasions. We spent the rest of the afternoon just relaxing and playing with the boys. After feeding them and putting them to bed we settled on the couch with a beer. I couldn't stop thinking about last night. It had been so long since I had been with anyone and being with Hawk had been amazing. I wanted more. Of course, we had to be careful with the boys' home not to get too loud. That's assuming he actually wants more of me. If that was a one-time thing, I would be so embarrassed. I decided to head to bed. Getting up I started to walk toward my room when Hawk took my hand and turned me around throwing me over his shoulder.

"You are sleeping with me." He said as he closed his door behind us. Setting me down on my feet he wrapped his hand around my neck and pulled me in for a kiss. I moaned into his mouth and pressed closer to him. Sliding my hands around his neck I slid my hands down his back and then back up pulling his shirt off. He moved back long enough to pull the shirt over his head and toss it away. Then his mouth was back on mine. I swear I could kiss him for hours. The way his tongue dueled with mine and when he sucked my lip into his mouth made my girl parts sing. He started to unsnap my jeans and I was helping him slide them down my legs, my shirt was suddenly gone, and I found myself on my back with him leaning over me. He looked into my eyes as he started to caress my body with his fingers. Sliding them across my collarbone, down my arm slowly. I squirmed under him, needing more. He smirked and started to kiss his way down my chest. He sucked my nipples into his mouth and nipped at them each in turn. I ran my hands down his back, enjoying the play of muscles and finding his ass. I loved a man with a nice ass. Nothing worse than flat ass on a man. I cupped the cheeks before he slid down my body effectively disengaging my hands and took my ass in his hands lifting me for his mouth. I raised up on my elbows as he licked me from bottom to top of my slit, eliciting a moan from me as I lay back down to just feel. He used his thumbs to spread me and started to flick the tip of his tongue on my clit. My thighs were trembling, and he slipped a finger into my channel then added a second one. Working his fingers in and out while he worked his tongue over and around my clit, I grabbed a pillow to cover my mouth as I came screaming into it. My body was convulsing around his fingers. He pulled them out and licked them clean. Prowling up my body he fit himself to my entrance and holding my hands above my head he slammed into me to the hilt. I bit my lip, and it sent me over again. He groaned at the feel of me coming around his cock. He pulled out and I moaned in protest.

"On your hands and knees." He told me and I scrambled to get into position. He slid back inside me and set a fast pace, taking us both back over with just a few thrusts. Once we caught our breath, he reached for a few tissues to clean us up before going for a damp washcloth. I went to the bathroom to take care of my nightly routine and then crawled back into the bed. He pulled me against his chest and spooned me from behind. I could get used to this.

9

Hawk

The rest of the week was pretty uneventful. I had to work the next few nights at the club, so I didn't get any alone time with Beth. She was still sleeping in my bed. I like to come home to her warming my bed. As soon as I got into the bed, she would find her way to my side to curl up to me. She was always up before me since she had to take care of the boys. Tonight was New Years Eve, and the club would be hopping. We had not seen any sign of the Italians hanging around lately. Maybe it was because Bethann had not been there. I hated that I had to work but the club would be closed tomorrow night for the holiday. The guys were having a party at the clubhouse, and they were bugging me to stop by after work. I had not been hanging out there much in the evenings. I had to leave for work in a few hours and Beth was putting the boys down for the night. Fang was watching the door for me until ten. The television was set at the New York Times Square Ball drop party, and we had a small bottle of champagne in the fridge. She came back into the living room, and I noticed she was wearing one of my T-shirts and nothing else.

"Love the outfit babe." I winked at her as she blushed. She wasn't one for dressing up much. I wanted to stay home with her, but I had heard that someone had reserved the VIP section at the club, and it was under the same Sartori. I wanted to be on hand in case there was trouble. Fury was going to be security for me as well. Gears and Doc were going to keep an eye on my place. It wasn't easy to get on our property, but I wouldn't say impossible.

"I didn't see any reason not to be comfortable since I would be curled up on the couch with a blanket and my champagne watching the ball drop on television." Beth looked at me up and down. I was really wishing I could stay home and just take her to bed. I crooked my finger at her, and she walked over to stand in front of me.

"I want you to keep the doors and windows locked up. You have my number as well as Axle's and a few others on speed dial. If you hear anything weird or feel uncomfortable, you call and one of the guys will come stay with you until I get home." I lifted her chin and kissed her lips. She pulled me closer and kissed me back.

"Wake me up when you get home, and we can finish this." She whispered in my ear. I held her in my arms for a few minutes and then got my coat. I wanted to scout the outside of the club and see if I needed to have any of the guys on the lookout. I was going to stop by Axle's place and find out what he wanted me to do about this mess. We did business with the Irish mafia out of Boston and sometimes the Russian Mafia in New York. We never dealt with the Italians. I knew we needed to tread carefully. I made sure to lock up on my way out and I had the security feed on my phone. I headed over to Axle's place. I knew he would be at the clubhouse later.

Knocking on his door, I heard him holler for me to come in. Walking inside I saw him watching a fight on tv with a beer in his hand.

"Grab a beer if you want." Axle said without looking away from the tv. "Got a call from Jackal."

I paused and turned to look at him. I had not heard that name in years. Jackal was part of the club in Boston. He was a good guy unlike most of the guys on the east coast. Snake, my father, was always trying to get a bigger piece of whatever they were doing. He wasn't to be trusted. Jackal kept an eye on things and reported to Axle when he could.

"What the fuck did he want?" I asked as I took a seat in a chair by the couch. I knew this wouldn't be good.

"Well seems they got a kid on the payroll that works at one of the restaurants owned by the Sartori Family. One where they hold their meetings in the back room. He overhead a conversation between Enzo and Vincente about a Candice that Enzo was living with and his kid. How she took off on him and cleaned out his safe at home. He was bragging that they found her and took care of her but had not found the kid yet." Axle cut his eyes over to me. "Obviously they don't know about the younger boy. I think it's a good move having Lillian keep them here on the property. The fewer people that see them out the better."

"I'm working Trixie's tonight. There is a table in the VIP section reserved under the name Sartori." I told him. He narrowed his eyes and drank the rest of his beer.

"I don't like the sound of that. I'm glad we got Bethann out of there when we did. I hate that she is going to be starting work the day after tomorrow, but it might be what we need to draw them out and end this mess."

"We are not using my girl as bait." I growled at him. "I do have extra eyes on her while she is working. Also, since she is working with Gears, I feel a little better about her having the job."

"It's good she is somewhere we can keep an eye on her. Make sure she knows to be extra cautious. No lunches alone and no leaving without someone walking her to her car." Axle got up and stretched turning off the tv. "I'm going to head over to the club for a bit. I have an itch to scratch. Catch me up tomorrow."

"Will do, have fun." I smirked at him as we walked out. Axle was a loner. He didn't do girlfriends and he only had sex with a few of the whores at the club. Only the ones who knew the score. He didn't deal with the clingy types. I watched him enter the clubhouse and I headed to my car so I could get to work.

I knew when I pulled up at Trixie's it was going to be a long night. There were two limos parked on the edge of the lot and they had New York plates. I walked over and placed a tracker on both cars before taking a picture and sending it over to James with Phoenix Security to have them check it out for me. I walked inside and nodded at Fury who was working the door tonight. Fang was in the corner near the stage, arms crossed looking at the VIP section. I glanced over and saw Enzo Sartori along with his minions, the Balducci cousins. They had a few of the strippers in their section giving them lap dances. I noticed that Enzo wasn't paying attention to the dancer in his lap but rather kept scoping the club looking for someone. I felt my fists clench knowing he was looking for Bethann. Since I helped to run the club, I took advantage of it and decided to introduce myself to our guests. As I cleared the velvet rope separating the couple of tables from the rest of the place his two goons stood up and crossed their arms. I sneered at them.

"Sir, this section is reserved you can't come up here." One of the cousins said to me. I raised my eyebrow at him.

"Actually, as I am part owner of the club, I go where I damn well please." I informed him as I stepped closer and placed my hand on my weapon. Technically the MC owned it, but as I was a charter member, that included me.

"Gentleman, you seem to be a long way from home. What brings you to our quaint little town on New Years' Eve?" I asked as I stopped at the table and focused on Enzo Sartori. "Seems a bit understated for you."

"We are looking for Candice Todd or her sister Bethann." He said smoothly, like he didn't already know Candy was dead. "I was told they worked here."

"They did, but not any longer." I said not offering any details. I wanted to see what they would reveal. I noticed the scowl on his face before he tried to school his features.

"I need to find them; Candice has something that belongs to me, and I want it back." He said focusing all his attention on me. "I'm not leaving town until I get it."

"Well, I guess you better get comfortable. Candy was killed a week before Christmas, so you won't be getting anything out of her." I told him. He didn't even blink when I said it.

"Do you happen to know where she was staying? Maybe her landlord would let me search the place to see if I can find it myself." He pulled out his wallet like he was about to offer me money. "I can make it worth your while."

"I don't need your money. Candy was our employee, so we took care of closing down her place and sending her things to her living relatives. I don't remember coming across anything that didn't belong to her." I said watching him closely. I saw him clench his fist and put his wallet back into his coat.

"What about her sister? I was led to believe she was your manager here." He started looking annoyed. "Maybe I could speak with her as Candice's last living relative to see if she has what I'm looking for."

"Ms. Todd no longer works here. She found another job that suits her much better." I said, trying not to give away that I knew where she was.

"Perhaps you could tell me where that is so that I may speak with her myself." Enzo said as he palmed his piece under his coat. I palmed mine as well.

"We do not share personal information about our past or present employees. I'm afraid you won't be getting any information here." I told him. I turned to leave, and his goons stepped in front of me. "You can either move out of my way on your own or you can be moved on a stretcher. Nobody threatens me in my place. I suggest you find somewhere else to party for the evening."

With a jerk of my head the dancers all filed out of the VIP area and dispersed to find other men to dance for. I stood by the door with Fury and watched as they left. I had the tracker information on my phone so I could keep tabs on them. I relieved Fury from the door so he could head to the party at the clubhouse, and I stood watch with Fang for the rest of the evening. I knew we had not seen the last of them.

10

*B*ethann

The temperature had dropped so I went and put on a pair of joggers and then curled up on the couch under a blanket with my e-reader. It was peaceful with the boys sleeping and since Hawk wasn't home, I couldn't sleep. I found a new book by one of my favorite romance authors and started to read. I had been really getting into the book when my phone rang. Figuring it was probably just Hawk checking on us, I answered it.

"*I want my kid and my money bitch. You will give them to me or else.*" The man said in an Italian accent and hung up. My hand was shaking as I put the phone down. I didn't want to bother Hawk at work. I was sure no one was going to get to us here. I wondered how he got my phone number. I got up and went to check on the boys. They were sound asleep. It occurred to me that he didn't know about Josh yet. He said kid singular. Once I was satisfied that they were not disturbed I checked the lock on their window and made sure the curtains were closed. I also checked the rest of the locks in the house. I decided to take a hot bath, hoping that would relax me enough to sleep. I found some bubble bath under the sink and poured a generous amount in the tub. Lighting a few candles, I turned off the overhead light and sank down into the steaming water. I brought my phone into the bathroom so that it wouldn't wake the boys if it rang again. I heard a beep and realized it was the alarm on the front door. I also realized the water had gone cold. I must have fallen asleep. I reached for the plug and then got out to dry off. I looked at my phone and it was half past two. I wrapped his robe around me and went into the bedroom to find Hawk standing there stripping off his clothes.

"Baby why aren't you asleep?" he said quietly. I shook my head and stripped off the robe crawling into bed. He climbed in beside me and pulled me close.

"I'm exhausted, can we talk about it when we wake up. Please?" I begged him. He looked at me and stroked my face gently leaning over to kiss me.

"Okay, but only because you look ready to drop." He kissed my head and I felt myself nodding off. I definitely needed sleep before I had to tell him about the phone call.

I woke up to a weight on my stomach and a little bouncing. I peeled open my eyes to see Cameron sitting on my stomach and Josh pushing on the bed. I looked over and Hawk was already up.

"Aunt Bethie, why are you in Mr. Hawks' room?" Cameron asked me. I didn't really want to try and explain that. I was about to say something when Hawk came in and scooped Josh off the floor with one arm and Cameron with the other.

"Time for waffles." He announced winking at me and taking them out of the room. I giggled and grabbed the robe to put on. I headed to my room to get dressed for the day. I was not looking forward to having this conversation with him. I entered the kitchen to find the boys already at the table with their waffles cut up and a sippy cup of milk in front of them. My plate was also sitting there with a cup of coffee and some juice. I smiled at him and shook my head.

"You shouldn't have done this. I could have fixed us breakfast. You worked last night." I fussed as I sat down.

"You had a rough night and I'm used to only getting five or six hours of sleep." He said as he took a bite of his own breakfast. I dove into my food, and it was delicious. He smiled at my obvious enjoyment. "You have your first day of work tomorrow at your new job. I wanted to do something nice for you today."

We ate while the boys chattered with mouthfuls of food. When they finished, I got them cleaned up and settled in the living room with some cartoons and a few toys. Pouring myself more coffee, I sat down and got ready to tell Hawk about the phone call.

"What's wrong? I know you were upset about something last night and I gave you a break since you were so tired. I want to know what happened to upset you like that." Hawk asked, taking my hand.

"I got a phone call last night around midnight. It was a man with an accent telling me he wanted his kid and his money or else. Then he hung up." I whispered looking at him. He squeezed my hand a bit and I could see the vein over his eye bulging a bit. "How did he get my number?"

"He was at the club last night with a few of his goons. They had some of the dancers with them. Are there any of the dancers that would give out your number?" he asked me with a frown. I tried to think if I had offended or pissed off any of them before I left. Brandi 'Bubbles' had been a bit hostile lately, but I couldn't think of any reason why she would be mad enough to give out my phone number.

"I don't think so. I did notice he said kid not kids, so he doesn't know about Josh. I was going to go get them some more clothes since they are starting to outgrow the ones they have. Thankfully Josh can wear some of Cam's hand me downs that don't fit anymore." I frowned thinking that I didn't want someone to see me buying two different sizes of clothes. The less they knew the better. "I also need some diapers and pull ups."

"Don't worry about that. We will place an overnight order for whatever you need. Let me see your phone so that I can get the number he called from. It's likely a burner phone but we want to see if we can trace it anyway." Hawk picked up my phone and looked at the missed call. He sent the number to his phone. "If you get any more calls, I want to know about them immediately and I would prefer you not answer. See if he will leave a voicemail."

"Okay, I can do that." I said as I watched my nephews playing, completely oblivious to the danger they were in. I would protect them both with my life and I knew Hawk would do the same. "You're a good man Sean Patrick McKay."

His eyes hardened a bit, and he shook his head. "I'm really not Beth. I have done things in the past that would make you run in the other direction." He got up and grabbed his jacket. "I'll be back before dinner." He said and he left.

I wondered what that was about. I don't care what he said. I know he is a good man. Perfect no, but good deep down for sure. I just had to help him see himself the way we see him. I looked through the fridge and cabinets to see what I could make for supper and then went to lay out clothes for work tomorrow. I was looking forward to seeing Sophie again. She seems really nice, and it would be nice to have some girlfriends. I have been a loner for such a long time.

11

Hawk

Driving around town, I kept an eye out for anything out of the ordinary. I could not stop thinking about the past. Bethann thinks I'm a good man, but if she knew some of the things my father had made me do in the past, she wouldn't be so quick to trust me. The Rippers' chapter in Boston was nothing like the one here in Liberty. It's a big part of why I relocated after my time in the service. They treated women like property and not the cherished kind. They took money from a lot of the local businesses for protection under orders from the Irish Mafia. Threatening to hurt the owner's family if they didn't agree to the arrangement. They gave us a nice cut and provided the club with women.

Renaldi's Diamonds was the nicest place in town and the owner had a beautiful daughter. She was nineteen and engaged to be married. Since they refused to pay, I was ordered to pick up the daughter and bring her to the clubhouse for the orgy they had every other Saturday night. I knew what they had planned for her. She would be passed around and used like a common whore, then they would dump her off in front of the store as a warning. I had done a lot of shit I wasn't proud of, but this really bothered me. I waited until the store opened the next day and went by the owners' home to get her. She answered the door thinking it was her fiancé. I put a cloth over her mouth and threw her over my shoulder. She was out and I laid her in the trunk of the car to take her to the club. When I got there, I brought her inside and put her in one of the rooms that locks from the outside. As she lay on the bed still passed out from the chloroform, I really looked at her. She had long black hair and an olive complexion like her father. I was pretty sure she was Italian. The more I looked at her the less I was on board with the plan. She was innocent and didn't deserve what the guys had planned for her. I just wasn't sure how I would get her out of there without them stopping me. I closed and locked the door and pocketed the key.

I jerked my head at my father and a few other guys. "I'll be back before the party starts." I told them and then I headed out. I knew if I did this, I would not be able to come back here. I headed to the recruitment office and signed up. I told them I needed to be gone by morning. After arrangements were made, I snuck back into the clubhouse and found they had already got in the room and were taking turns with her. She was screaming and crying, I was about to pull the last one off of her when he punched her in the face, and I heard her neck crack. Her eyes rolled back in her head, and she wasn't breathing anymore. I backed out of the room and grabbed my duffle and left. I never looked back.

I met Fury and Rider while I was in Afghanistan, we served together. They told me about the Rippers in Liberty, and I told them about the ones in Boston. When we finished our tour, they invited me back to Liberty to meet their Pres and see if I could be patched in with them. Undertaker had me start off as a prospect and made me earn my patch in their club. I was completely honest about where I came from and what I had done before. They all accepted me, and we never spoke of it. I just hoped that Bethann would be able to accept it. I have turned my life around since coming here. I try to atone for the Renaldi girl with every action I take. Bethann was someone I had been interested in for months before her sister was killed and there was no way I was going to let her fall victim to her sister's bad choices. I would protect her and those boys with my life.

Pulling up at the diner, I went in for a cup of coffee. I knew Beth was making dinner so I would not disrespect her by having dinner here. I just needed to get my head on straight before heading back home. I looked up and saw Undertaker, Annie and Mattie at a booth near the back. I went over to speak to them.

"Hey Annie, when are you gonna leave this old man and run away with me." I winked at her as Undertaker growled. She giggled and shook her head at me.

"Never gonna happen Hawk. I just got him trained, besides I'm pretty sure Bethann wouldn't take to kindly to that." Annie grinned at me as she fed a broken-up fry to little Mattie.

"What are you doing here?" Undertaker asked as he moved over so I could sit down. "I figured you would be at home with your girl and her nephews."

"I'm heading home soon. I just needed to get out of my head some." I said as I watched his little boy playing with the fries. He was a cute little thing, looked just like Undertaker.

"Son, you have got to let go of the past. You have built a new family here with us. We have your back. Let it go, you deserve to be happy." He said as he slapped me on the shoulder. "You have punished yourself enough."

"I guess. I am going to leave you to your dinner. I should head back; Bethann was going to be cooking dinner. I don't want to be late. When things settle down you should bring Mattie over to play with the boys. I'm sure Cam and Josh would love to have a playmate." I smiled and kissed Annie on top of her head and left.

I drove by the firm where Bethann would be working and scoped it out. I wanted to know every way in or out of the place. I had a tracker placed in her new phone and one in a pair of earrings I was going to give her tonight to celebrate her new job. I glanced at my watch and headed for the compound.

Pulling up to the gate I saw Fury sitting outside talking to Lillian. She looked annoyed at him. I wondered what that was about but not enough to ask. He looked frustrated and he walked off. I drove to my place and parked. As I walked through the door, I saw Bethann fixing the boys plates. I headed to the sink to wash my hands.

"Hey baby, something smells amazing." I said watching her blush. "Sorry I was gone so long. I ran into Undertaker and Annie and got to talking. Have seat and I'll fix your plate." Taking her by the waist I eased her into a chair and leaned over to give her a kiss. After fixing our plates I sat down to join them.

"It's okay, we just played with their cars, and I fixed dinner. They will be going to bed after their bath, they had short naps today." she said as she took another bite and glanced over at me. The boys looked like they were about to pass out in their supper. "I'm looking forward to work tomorrow. I hate feeling so dependent for everything."

"I know you are very independent, and I respect that. This wasn't your doing though. You didn't choose for any of this to happen so cut yourself a break. We will get through this. I'm happy to provide whatever you and the boys need." I told her fiercely. I didn't want her to feel like a burden. "You also don't have to cook dinner every night. I'm capable of cooking for us as well."

"I don't mind, it makes me feel useful. Now that I'm going back to work, we can trade off." She suggested as she stood to clear the table. I stopped her by placing my hand on top of hers.

"Why don't you go bathe the boys and I'll clean up the kitchen." Bethann smiled and gave me a nod. I watched as she picked Josh up out of his highchair and helped Cam down from his booster seat. She was so good with her nephews; she was going to be a great mother to them. I wondered if she would want any of her own. Lord, I'm forty-five years old and I'm thinking about having kids. Laughing at my thoughts, I got up to clean the kitchen. She may not even want to be with me in the long-term. I would have to court her and show her that we can be happy together.

12

Bethann

The boys were exhausted so I gave them a quick bath and got them ready for bed. After getting them settled and reading a bedtime story they were out. I left their lamp on and eased out of the room pulling the door closed quietly. As I walked into the living room, I saw Hawk sitting on the couch and in front of him was a jeweler's bag. I looked at him and raised an eyebrow. He chuckled when he saw my reaction.

"It won't bite. It's just a little gift to congratulate you on your new job." He said watching me sit down beside him. I reached for the bag and pulled out a small box. I gasped as I opened it and saw a beautiful pair of diamond earrings surrounded by aquamarine stones.

"This is too much, Hawk. I can't accept these." I told him as he shook his head and proceeded to put them on me.

"You deserve beautiful things. I would be honored if you would wear these. They reminded me of those beautiful eyes of yours." He said as he leaned back to admire them in my ears. I put my arms around his neck and crawled into his lap. I leaned in to kiss him and he put his hands on either side of my face while he kissed and nibbled on my lips then trailed kisses down my neck pulling me into a kneeling position so he could kiss lower. Raising back up he looked in my eyes and said, "Let's take this to our bedroom." I stood up and took his hand walking toward his room. He closed the door behind us and pulled his shirt off over his head. I licked my lips; I would never get tired of looking at his chest. Seriously, the man was a work of art. He took care of his body, and it showed in all the ridges on his abs and the muscles that played beneath his golden skin. I wanted to take my time kissing and licking all over that chest of his. He smirked as he unbuttoned his jeans and slid them down his legs along with his briefs. Biting my lip, I pulled my own sweater off and shimmied my jeans down my legs kicking them away. He stalked toward me with a wicked gleam in his eyes. With a little push I fell back onto the bed and scooted myself back until he grabbed my legs and threw them over his massive shoulders.

"I didn't get any dessert after dinner. I want something sweet." He said as he took a swipe with his tongue through my soaked folds. "Delicious." he said before burying his face in my pussy and eating me like I was his last meal. I writhed on the bed, and he placed an arm over my abdomen to hold me down. I could feel myself getting close and then he focused on my clit flicking his tongue over and around it before sucking on it hard sending me over the edge. I shoved a pillow over my mouth to keep from crying out, so I didn't see him move until I felt him thrust into me.

"Damn baby, your still having contractions from your orgasm. It feels amazing." He moaned as he kept thrusting while holding my legs up on either side of his shoulders. He licked and kissed my ankle while he fucked me, and I never knew that was an erogenous zone. I started to go over the edge when he picked up his speed sending us both over the edge. Gently he eased my legs down and pulled out of me. Grabbing tissues to keep from making too big of a mess.

"That was amazing. I can't move now." I laughed as I lay there completely spent. I was a little disappointed that I didn't get a chance to explore his body. I was going to have to do that in the morning sometime. He came back in with a warm washcloth and cleaned me up before pulling the covers back and helping me under them. "Can you throw me your shirt? I can't sleep nude with the boys in the house." He tossed his shirt and then climbed into the bed beside me.

"I'll have to work the next few nights at the club." He whispered in my ear as he spooned me from behind. "Tomorrow night I'm going to get us take out, so you don't have to cook."

I was all warm and cozy, falling asleep so I just gave a little mumble and let myself drift off.

The next morning, I woke up to the smell of coffee and bacon cooking. I crawled out of bed and took a quick shower before getting dressed. I went to the kitchen to see the boys at the table eating eggs, bacon and toast. Hawk was already dressed and placed a cup of coffee at the table for me. I walked over and gave him a kiss on the cheek. He wrapped and arm around my waist, leaned down and kissed me on the lips.

"Good morning. Lillian will be here in about fifteen minutes. I packed your lunch for work. I don't want you going out alone." He said as he fixed our plates and put them on the table. We sat down to eat and by the time we were finished I heard Lillian knock at the door. The boys were excited to see her. I was glad they were comfortable with her. It made it easier to leave them to go to work. I kissed the boys and put my coat on as Hawk handed me my purse and my lunch while walking me out to my car. "Baby, please be very careful and aware of your surroundings. Text me when you get to work and are inside and then again when you leave."

"I will, thank you for fixing my lunch. That was very sweet." I told him as I kissed him on the lips before getting into my car to go. He opened the door, and my car was warm and running. I smiled at him as he leaned inside buckling my seatbelt and kissing me again. He was so thoughtful.

"Have a good day baby." Hawk said as he closed my door and stepped back. I knew he would be doing stuff around the clubhouse today until he came home for dinner before work tonight. I pulled out and saw Gears behind me. Looks like I have an escort to work.

It was a short drive to the office, and I pulled up beside Austin. I have to remember to call him that. He got out and walked around to let Sophie out of the car. They were so sweet together. I sent a quick text off to Hawk to let him know I was here, and that Austin was walking me in.

"Good morning, Bethann. Welcome to H & W Accounting." Austin said as he unlocked the front door for us to go in. They stopped at the reception desk, and I put my purse down on the chair. "This is your desk; we will get the rest of your hiring paperwork out of the way. Sophie will help train you since we had to fire the previous receptionist. I'm sure you will do fine. I have some calls to return and it's always a little crazy after the holiday."

Austin went into his office and closed the door. I turned to Sophie, who had been watching her guy before he closed the door.

"Right, so put your purse in the bottom left drawer of your desk and then follow me. We have half an hour before we are actually open. Let's get some coffee and I'll show you where you can keep your lunch." Sophie said as I followed her back to the kitchen/break area. "We keep the bottom shelf stocked with bottled water and sodas. If there is something particular you like send me an email and I'll be sure to add it. We offer clients coffee or a cold beverage when they arrive and usually put them in one of the two conference rooms before announcing their arrival. Right now, most of the accounts are handled by Austin or me. Mr. Heath is taking a bit of a break to be with his wife. She is having twins. You will meet him when he comes in for the weekly meeting. We have those on Friday mornings."

The rest of the morning was spent with Sophie showing me the ropes and finishing up paperwork. I caught on quickly to the system and fell into a routine for the day. The job was not hard, and I hoped to get more responsibilities later after I had proven myself. Sophie was a joy to work with. She told me that it would be a little slower the next couple of weeks until all the tax forms started coming in and people got ready to have their taxes done. Around noon they locked the door for lunch break. I went to get my lunch out. Hawk had fixed me a Turkey and bacon sandwich with tomato and lettuce on the side to add. There was an apple and a bag of chips. I saw a note at the bottom of the bag and blushed. I opened the note to read to myself.

Baby,
Have a great first day at work. I know you will do great.
H.

I folded it back up and placed it in my purse and ate the lunch he packed for me. Austin joined us for lunch but ate quickly and said he had a lot to catch up on. I think he just wanted to give Sophie and I a chance to chat.

"So, I have been dying to ask how it is going with Hawk. I just met everyone this past month. He seems so rough around the edges." Sophie asked. "I mean they have all been so kind to me, he just doesn't talk much."

"It helps that I used to run Trixie's, their strip club. It is a legitimate business. My sister was a dancer before she was killed. Anyway, I have known most of the guys for a couple of years from work. Hawk works the door as security, so we have a history." I told her as I nibbled on my sandwich. "Things seem to be going well with you and Austin."

"Yes, he is wonderful. I wish I had not waited so long to give him a chance." She said smiling to herself. "I have never been so happy. Now if I could just find someone for my best friend Cara. She works too much."

"We should all have a get together. You, me, your friend Cara, Lillian and Annie. We could do it at Hawks place. He works nights so he is gone from eight to two on the nights he is at the club. Annie could put Mattie down with Josh and Cam." I suggested to her.

"Sounds like a great idea. I'll talk to Austin, and we will make plans." Sophie tossed her trash, and we headed back to our desks to finish out the day.

13

Hawk
I knew Bethann was excited to have a job again and that she didn't like being dependent on me. I just wanted to keep her safe. She has always been a hard worker and very independent. I almost wanted the Italians to make their move so we could put an end to this. I hated that they were taking their time. I knew they weren't stupid, but it seems if he wanted Cameron they could have gone after him legally. No, I'm sure it's the missing money he wants. Beth had not received any more messages since the first one. I felt sure that there would be more coming. She jumped every time her phone rang. I hated to see her scared. I'm wondering if he was skimming money from the family. Vincente is known for being ruthless, but he isn't crazy. Enzo, on the other hand, is known for his greed and cruelty. I'm betting he was trying to get information out of Candy and lost his temper. Now Bethann is his only connection to the money. He will try to use his son to get what he wants from her. I'm not going to let that happen.

I rounded up a couple of the guys and we went hunting for any of them we could squeeze for information. He had a couple of lower-level guys hanging around watching the club, but we had banned them from coming inside. I had noticed the car driving by the past week, but it only came by around closing and didn't stop. I think they were looking to see if Bethann was leaving after a shift. We told them she no longer worked there but they didn't believe us. I got my text from Beth this morning and I know that Gears will call if anything happens.

My phone rang, I looked and saw it was Fury. I pulled over and called him back.

"Did you find something?" I asked him. I heard something muffled in the background and then the crunch of knuckles to a face. It's a sound you never forget.

"Yeah, got one of those scumbags hanging around the diner across from her job. We have him in the basement of the clubhouse. Keeping him warm for you." He said sarcastically. Knowing Fury, he was working him over already. He enjoyed hurting people like that.

"Be there in ten." I hung up and headed back to the compound. I wanted information. When I arrived, I pulled behind the clubhouse and went down to the back entrance. It looked like a cold storage, and it was, just not for food. We had it soundproofed so no one could hear the screams. While we tried to stay as legit as possible there were times when we had to torture information out of traitors. I knocked on the inner door and Blade opened up. I saw Fury standing there with his favorite set of chains around his neck dripping with blood. He had a way of using them and not for securing someone. Nope he used them like a weapon. I never wanted to be on the receiving end of those chains. He looked over at me and nodded.

"I found pictures of your girl on his phone; he had sent them to Enzo. They were planning to grab her after work. I already alerted Gears. He will bring her home. He also bragged about what he wanted to do to her after they found the money. I think we should use him to send a message to that Italian scum." Fury growled as he used his chains to break the man's leg.

"Did you see any messages to Vincente from the scum?" I asked Fury. He shook his head. "I think we should call him and tell him what his brother is up to." The man's eyes got wider and he looked even more afraid. I watched his expression. "He doesn't know about Enzo and the money, does he?" I asked the man in the chair. He shook his head.

"Vincente will kill my family if he finds out I betrayed him. Enzo was going to give me the girl and a promotion. He plans to kill his brother. The money was to buy himself some loyalty. The girl must have found it and took it when she left." He was crying now, and it just pissed me off.

"So not only is he a piece of shit who abuses women, but he is disloyal to his family and is planning his own brother's murder?" I asked him. "You may as well tell us. You're going to die anyway. It can be quick, or I can let Fury keep playing with you."

"Yes, yes he plans to murder his brother and take over the family. He has several men that are loyal to him. They were going to make it look like the Irish killed him. He has a man on his payroll from Boston that works with the Irish Mafia, so he has information to help him." The man was squealing like a pig at this point.

"Did you hear a name?" I asked him as I played with my knife. He whimpered as I moved closer with it.

"Snake, the guy is with an MC in Boston." I stopped dead in my tracks when I heard him say that name. I had not heard that name since I left Boston and joined the Marines. My fucking father was a traitor. I think we are going to have to clean house soon. "That's all I know."

I noticed there was plastic underneath him, so I went over and cut his throat. I wiped my knife off his clothes and put it back in my pocket.

"Get rid of the body after you get his ID out of his pocket. I need to know who he is when we make the call to his boss. I'm going to ask Axle for a club meeting." I left and headed to my house. I knew that she would be home soon, and Gears was bringing her. I called and ordered a few pizzas to be delivered and went to relieve Lillian. I shot off a text to the pres and went inside. It was almost four and Gears said they would be leaving work in about half an hour. I sent Bethann a text asking her to ride home with Gears and Sophie. I wanted to take a shower before she got home. Lillian looked up from the couch where she was reading to the boys as I walked in. She glanced at me and saw the blood on my shirt raising an eyebrow. Her old man was member, so she knew what went on. We didn't give our women details, but they weren't stupid.

"I'm going to shower before Bethann gets home. When I get out you can head on home." I told her. She nodded and went back to the story. Her old man Wolf had been a good friend of mine. It sucked that she had to lose him so early, but it was a part of life. She still had a home here with us and the guys were her family.

I stripped off my clothes and took a shower. When I got out, I made sure to put my clothes in the washer and start it. I didn't want Bethann to clean blood out of my clothes. I heard the doorbell and headed to answer it. I knew it was our dinner. I took the pizza and put it in the kitchen. Pulling out a couple of slices to cool down for the boys. Lillian got her stuff and left. I fixed the boys a sippy cup of milk each and got them settled. I heard the door a few minutes later and saw Bethann come inside with a worried look on her face. She smiled when she saw the boys at the table eating. I fixed her a plate and a drink so we could sit down and eat with them. Laying her purse on the couch she walked over and kissed me as well as both boys before sitting down to eat.

"How was your first day?" I asked her, trying to keep the conversation light in front of the kids. She smiled at me.

"It was good. I enjoy working with Sophie. The job isn't hard but there is plenty to do. We were talking about getting the girls together for drinks one night." She said taking a bite of her pizza. I didn't like the idea of them going out anywhere right now. She must have read the look on my face because she shook her head. "Here, we were going to have them here. Since you work nights, they could come here, and we can hang out after the boys go to bed. I knew you wouldn't want me to go to a bar or anything while everything was still up in the air."

I relaxed when she said that. It showed that she would be a great old lady. She understood about safety and taking precautions. I was thankful that she wasn't pouting or having a fit to do what she wants.

"Hopefully we can resolve this soon and you and the girls can have a real lady's night." I told her as I squeezed her hand. "I hate that I have to go to work tonight, I'd much rather be here with you."

"I know but someone needs to mind Trixie's." she winked at me. I wanted to be worthy of her so bad. While I missed seeing her at work, this was so much better because I got to sleep beside her and wake up beside her. I loved having her and the boys here in my home. It's like the family I never thought I would have.

"Hey boys, how about we go play with your cars while your Aunt Bethie takes a bath." I got a damp paper towel to clean their hands off and then carried them off to the living room. "I'll clean up the dinner dishes after I get them settled."

"Thanks, a bath sounds nice." She said as she went to our room and closed the door. I sat on the floor playing with them and Josh settled on my lap leaning against me playing with one of his cars. Cameron was pushing his car along the tracks that I set up in the corner of the room for them. I believed in having the kids play in the room with us. Kids should know they are loved and be around the parents. I didn't believe in sending them to their rooms to play all the time. Besides, I enjoyed watching them. I felt Josh slump over, so I carried him to their room and put on his jammies then tucked him into bed. Cameron came in with us, so he was sitting on his bed waiting for his pajamas. I got him ready for bed and then sat on his bed with him tucked into me and was reading him Curious George. It was his favorite book. I heard a noise and looked up from the book to see Bethann leaning against the door frame smiling at us. She had on one of my T-shirts and a pair of my boxers with her hair down one side in a loose braid. I finished reading the book and Cameron rolled over and tucked his stuffed monkey into his arms. He was asleep in minutes. I eased out of the bed and leaned over to tuck his covers around him kissing him on his head. I walked to the door and Beth backed up to allow me to close the door.

"You're so good with them. They are crazy about you." She said as she sat in my lap on the couch. She absently rubbed her hand on my chest as she laid her head on my shoulder. "Do you want to tell me what happened today that made you want Austin to bring me home?"

I kissed her head and rubbed her back. I didn't want to scare her, but I wouldn't lie or keep things from her. I wanted a relationship with this woman and honesty was the best way to go.

"You were being watched. Fury noticed a guy at the diner across from the firm taking pictures with his phone and watching the door. He took him for a ride. We found pictures of you entering work this morning and some of the front desk. He also sent those pictures to his boss. We took care of him but there is a situation we have to handle. I'm working on getting a meeting of the club officers together so we can discuss a plan." I told her and felt her sigh. "I'm sorry baby. I won't let him hurt you."

"I know you won't. I don't want you to get hurt either. These people are dangerous." She looked up at me with worry in her beautiful eyes. "I care about you."

"Baby I am crazy about you. You are it for me." I told her. "I am crazy about those boys too. I'll do everything I can to keep the three of you safe." She stroked my jaw and leaned up to kiss me. Looking at the clock I saw it was almost seven. I didn't have time to start anything since I needed to get to work. I pulled her close and kissed her back.

"We will have to pick this up later baby. I have to go to work and if I start, I'm going to want hours to finish." I told her, kissing her nose and then sitting her on the couch. "Get plenty of rest. Gears will pick you up for work in the morning. I'll have one of the guys pick your car up tonight and bring it home."

"Ok. Be safe." She said as she turned on the television to one of her shows. I left and locked up behind me. I had to find out what my father was up to. They didn't call him Snake for nothing. He was a slippery bastard. I had hoped I would never have to see him again. Looks like I'm not going to be that lucky. I checked the schedule. Fang would already be at the club. He was doing a great job running it. The ladies loved him. The whole silver fox thing worked for Fang. He was divorced, his wife ran off on him years ago with a younger man. She was a real bitch, so he was better off without her. Since then, he gets what he needs from the women who hang around the club and doesn't give them the time of day otherwise. The dancers know how to give him a wide berth at work. The ones who attend the parties fight over who gets him that night. Apparently, the man is hung and knows how to please them. Nothing I want to know about. I have had my share of the women who frequent the parties. I have not touched anyone since

I took Bethann into my home. I didn't want anyone else. I'm no saint, I was balls deep in a whore the night her sister died but all that stopped when I realized she was actually interested in me. I was almost off the property when a 911 text came through to meet at Axle's house now. I turned and headed to his place. Fang messaged that he had one of the other bouncers watching so he could come to the meet.

14

*H*awk

I walked up to the door and knocked. Axle opened it and nodded for me to come in. Most of the guys were already here. We were just waiting on Fang. Axle had a long table that seats eight. This was perfect for the officers. When Fang came in, we all sat around the table to start the meeting.

"I got a message to Vincente Sartori that I wanted to meet with him. I don't trust having this conversation over the phone. He agreed to come here. His brother thinks he is heading to the Caymans for a few days off. He chartered a private plane to Denver, and we will meet him there at the Hilton by the Airport. I told him we had some information he needed and that we would only disclose it in person. He will have two of his trusted guys and I will have Fury and Hawk with me. I know this is not our usual style but the fact that he is willing to come so far to meet us shows respect, so we are doing this his way. I am assured his brother will not be there and knows nothing. It will be in two days; we will drive up there and then come back right after the meeting. Hopefully with a plan to end Enzo Sartori. I will be taking the money from the safe. It is likely the only way to trade for Bethann and the boy's safety. I'll have Undertaker and Gears keeping an eye out."

"I'd feel better if they all stayed in the clubhouse and the single guys stayed as well. No one is getting in there. Also, more room for a few of the guys to keep watch." I said as I looked around. The guys nodded.

"I live there anyway so I'm happy to keep an eye out for your girl and the kids." Rider said. Blade and Doc agreed.

"Okay that's settled. I'll have Lillian keep the boys there the day we go, and Gears will bring her to the clubhouse after work." Hawk said.

"Bear said he and a couple of the guys from Phoenix Security will patrol around town. Keep an eye out for Enzo and his minions." Axle said. "Nobody not in the club or directly related comes on this property until this is over, understood?" Everyone agreed.

We all left, Fang and I headed to Trixie's to work our shift. I hoped this would be over soon. I really hated that my father was involved and the idea that I may have to see him again made me want to hit something. I needed to make a call later to one of my old friends in the O'Leary Family. Collum O'Leary used to be my best friend. He knew what a bastard my father was. They used the Rippers MC in Boston as muscle. Since Collum took over as the head of the family they had less to do with the Rippers. He knew what they were up there, and he didn't trust them. My father just made a grave mistake thinking he could double cross Collum. I would be getting word to him. It would also buy us some favor with the family. Everything was business as usual at Trixie's. Dancers were doing their thing, and the customers were staying in line. I checked the bar, and the drinks were flowing. The bouncers had everything under control.

"Boss, one of those Italian pricks tried to get in when you and Fang left. He is cooling his heels in the basement." Mick said as he kept a watch on the stage. He was a good guy and had proven to be a good employee. I had thought to have him pledge for the club, but not until all the rats were put away. I was not taking any chances with the safety of the women and children that lived on the compound.

"Good job. I'll have Fury come talk to him. Head on over to the bar area and watch the side stage." I told him as I took my place by the door. I sent a text to Fury that we had more fun waiting for him downstairs. We would wait until after close to go down and 'talk' to him.

About closing time, I see Bubbles headed my way. I really didn't want to deal with her tonight. She makes her first mistake by rubbing up to me and trying to kiss me. I set her away from me.

"No." I said firmly. She gave me a pout and pushed out her chest. Sadly for her, Bethann's was better and real. I had no reaction to this girl at all.

"You used to like to fuck me. Why don't you want me anymore?" she whined. I looked at her and wondered why I ever touched her in the first place. She was as fake as they come. Too much makeup, dyed hair and fake boobs. Nothing compared to my Bethann, fresh faced, long natural blonde hair and real boobs. She was everything I ever wanted in a woman. This here, this was what I wasted time with.

"I never wanted you in particular. I just needed a wet hole to put my cock. I'll never touch you again. If you try this even one more time your fired." I said and looked over at Mick who nodded his head. "Go home."

Fury walked in a few minutes later and looked at me wrinkling his nose. "You smell like a whore. Bubbles?" I grunted.

"Unfortunately, she doesn't understand the word no." I muttered. "We have work downstairs. Let's go." Fury chuckled. He followed me down to the basement. Fang locking up and coming right behind us. When we got downstairs there was a light on and an Italian man tied to an iron chair. The floor was tiled with a drain. We had that added after we bought the club. It was also soundproof and a good place to keep enemies.

"I remember him, this one was with Enzo the night they came to the club, and we kicked them out." I told my brothers. "Tell me, where is that little shit of a boss you follow around like a puppy?"

"I won't tell you anything, I'm sure my cousin has your girl and Enzo's brat by now." He spat at me.

"You think so? Fury, show him the picture of our guest." I said watching for the man's reaction. Fury pulled up the picture of the guy he worked over that he took beforehand. The man's face blanched. Then Fury showed him a picture of what was left before they got rid of the body. The man threw up. I pulled out my phone and checked my cameras. My woman was asleep on the couch and the boys were sound asleep in their beds.

"You, murdering bastards, you killed my cousin. I hope Enzo rapes the girl over and over. I hope he shares her with his men." He hissed. I backhanded him. Then I looked over my shoulder. Fury pulled his chain off and smiled. It was his wicked, I can't wait to hurt you, smile.

"My girl is safe and asleep in my house with her nephew. You will never touch her, and neither will your filthy boss." I told him. "I get first crack at him." I stripped off my shirt and hung it up. Pulling out my knife. Walking over to him, I carved the word pussy into his chest. "You wanted to hurt people I care about. You wanted to rape her and share her. Now I'm going to carve you and share you." I stabbed him in the crotch with my knife. "He's all yours, Fury. Make sure ya'll get rid of him when your done having your fun with him."

I headed home. We would be meeting with the head of the Sartori Family in two days. I needed some rest. We have taken out Enzo's two closest minions. Now we needed to find that little bastard. I wanted to deliver him to his brother as the traitor he is. I have heard what Vincente does to traitors. As I pulled up to the house it was close to dawn. I needed a shower before I crawled into bed with my girl. I didn't want any of this filth to touch her. I turned off the alarm and unlocked the door entering as quietly as I could since I knew she was asleep on the couch. After resetting the alarm, I went to shower.

15

Bethann

It was the cold air coming through the front door that woke me up. I saw Hawk head straight for our room. I knew he was going to shower. I looked at the clock and saw that it was almost five in the morning. Trixie's closed at two and the latest he should have been home was three. I decided I didn't want to know where he was, if he was going to go off and fuck other women after work then I damn sure wouldn't be sleeping in his bed. I went to my room and crawled into my bed. I knew I wouldn't be sleeping but I needed him to know that I wasn't a doormat. If he wanted to fuck other women, then he wouldn't be fucking me. I smelled the cloying perfume on him when he passed the couch. It smelled like the shit Bubbles liked to wear. I knew he had been with her before so it shouldn't be any surprise that he would go back for more. I lay in bed staring at the ceiling, tears streaming down my face. I heard the shower cut off and then a few minutes later I heard Hawk go into the living room. A few minutes later he came into my room.

"Why are you in here?" he asked me. "I know you're not asleep, you were just on the couch. So why are you not in our bed."

"I'm not sleeping with a man who has been fucking another woman. You came in reeking of that bitch's perfume." I hissed at him as I wiped my eyes. "The club closed almost three hours ago, and I know it doesn't take three hours to cash out the dancers and servers."

"You're right, it doesn't. What does take several hours is interrogating someone. I spent the last several hours interrogating the other one of Enzo's people who has been stalking you." He said looking angry.

"So, you're telling me that's why you smell like a whorehouse?" I screeched at him. He walked over to me and put his hands on my arms picked me up and put me in his lap.

"No, Bubbles can't take no for an answer, so she tried to get in my pants again tonight. I told her if she touched me again, I would fire her. Then I went down to take care of the little bastard that wanted to hurt what is mine." Hawk said as he held me tight to his chest. "Instead of asking me where I was, you accuse me of cheating on you. Have I given you any reason to doubt me?"

I looked into his eyes and the hurt I saw there made me feel ashamed of my accusations. This man has had my back from the beginning. He deserved the benefit of the doubt. He deserved to be asked where he was and what he was doing. I felt tears streaming down my face again. Hawk held me in his arms as I cried.

"I'm sorry, I'm so sorry. Please forgive me." I said looking up at him. "I was jealous and insecure. I hated every one of those women that had been with you. I hated the ones that looked at you with fuck me eyes. I wanted to scratch them out of their heads."

"Baby, I never knew you cared. You never gave me any indication that you liked me until you were living under my roof. I'd have given up the women the first time I saw you if you had given me one word or look to tell me you were interested." Hawk said, as he looked at me in wonder.

"I was too proud. I saw what happened to my sister for loving the wrong man and I didn't really know you. I should have known better this morning." I stared at my hands because I was afraid to look into his eyes and see the disappointment. He lifted my chin to look in my eyes.

"I'm not going anywhere, and I don't want anyone else. Please talk to me next time you feel doubts creeping in. You have to get up in about two hours. Let's take a nap so you will feel more rested for work. Gears will pick you up." He laid back on the bed and pulled me down into his arms. I was so tired from crying I fell asleep in his arms.

A few hours later I was at work when a delivery guy came in with a dozen black roses. He looked around and set them on the desk. Before I could ask who they were for, he took off. I looked at the bouquet and saw a card peeking out. I reached for it and opened the card.

I WANT MY MONEY BITCH... I'LL BE AT THE DINER TOMORROW AT NOON. BRING THE MONEY OR I KILL THE KID.

I dropped the card and was shaking. I reached for my phone to call Hawk. I hated to wake him up, but he would be upset if I didn't. He picked up on the second ring.

"Baby, what's wrong?" Hawk asked calmly. I couldn't seem to get the words out. Suddenly Gears was behind me, he took the phone. Sophie hugged me.

"Hey man, there was a flower delivery and a note attached. It's a threat for Cam to Bethann. I'm giving her the rest of the week off. Come get her." Gears told Hawk. "She will stay right here with Sophie and myself until you get here."

"Okay honey, why don't you come with me to my office. Sophie, please lock the door, and put up the closed sign. Hawk will call when he gets here." Gears told them and then led the girls to his office to wait.

"I'm sorry, you must regret hiring me. My first week and I make it less than a couple of days." I have my head in my hands, elbows on my knees. I feel like such a burden. Suddenly I heard banging on the door. Gears goes to check it out. Hawk comes in and picks me up sitting down with me in his lap. Rubbing my back and murmuring soothing words. This man really is my rock.

"Baby, where is the note." Hawk asked gently. Gears handed it to him. He looked it over and I felt him tense up. "We are supposed to meet with Vincente Sartori tomorrow afternoon in Denver. You and the boys will be staying at the clubhouse with Lillian and several of the guys. It's the safest place while I am out of town. We are not staying overnight. Just driving up for the meeting and then coming back home."

I looked at him and I couldn't hide the fear on my face. I didn't want anything to happen to him. I was also nervous being that far away from him right now. He made me feel safe. I knew he was trying to make us safe so I couldn't complain. I just lay my head down on his shoulder and tried to calm my breathing.

"Ok, we will do whatever you say. I just want this to be over." I said quietly. "Can we go home now?"

"Sure, baby lets go home. Gears, it's probably a good idea for all of us to head back." Hawk helped me stand and then took my hand to lead me out to his car. We pulled up to his house and went inside. The boys were down for their afternoon nap and Lillian was watching one of her shows. She looked up worried when she saw us come in early.

"Is everything okay?" Lillian asked as she turned off the television and looked at me.

"Sartori sent Bethann some flowers with a threat. The good news is that we may be able to use this. You know I can't tell you anymore. Why don't you take the rest of the day off. I'll have ya'll staying at the clubhouse tomorrow. We have to go to Denver for a few hours." Hawk looked back at me. "I'm going to run her a bath and take care of dinner. We will see you tomorrow around ten."

"I'll see you all tomorrow." Lillian slipped on her coat and her purse then left. I took off Bethann's coat and purse then led her to the bathroom.

"Shower or bath?" he asked me. I nodded to the shower. I was just mentally and physically exhausted from the scare. He reached in and started the water then turned back to undress me. Hawk stripped down and got in with me to make sure I didn't fall. Gently washing me and helping me dry off before putting me to bed.

"I'll wake you up in a couple of hours for dinner. Don't worry about the boys, I got them." Hawk told me as he tucked me in. Leaning over he gently kissed my lips then my forehead. I felt myself drifting off.

16

Hawk

I hated seeing my girl so scared. I knew she loved those boys like they were her own and so did I. Enzo didn't know about Josh, but they were always together so a threat to one was a threat to both. I was not letting him get his hands on any of them. We were meeting with Vincente in less than twenty-four hours. Maybe we will have yet another bargaining tool to take with us tomorrow. If we can get our hands on Enzo, we could deliver him to his brother. I called Axle and told him what happened. I needed a couple of the guys to help set him up tomorrow. Maybe we could get a decoy. I didn't want to use Bethann as bait. We would be thinking of our options and decide in the morning.

I looked in on the boys and they were playing quietly. I knew they would be more rambunctious once they were more comfortable here. I wanted them to know this was home. I checked Josh's diaper, got him changed and Cameron went to the bathroom like a big boy. I put them at the table with a couple of their cars as well as a snack, while I fixed dinner. I wanted my girl to get some much-needed rest. I was making spaghetti since it was easy, and I always had ground beef on hand.

I had dinner ready when I saw Bethann come out of the bedroom. She had pulled her long hair up in a ponytail and had on some leggings and one of my hoodies. She smiled at her nephews as she kissed them both on the head and then put her arms around my waist from behind. I squeezed her hands that were on my abs and enjoyed the feeling of her pressed against me.

"Will you fix us both a drink while I fix our plates?" I asked her and she stepped around me to get glasses. The boys had drinks, so she just refilled theirs. I had their spaghetti cut up and cooled off. "You feel any better after your nap?"

"Aunt Bethie, you took a nap too?" Cam asked her with his eyes big. "I didn't think growned ups tooks naps?

"Sometimes they do peanut, sometimes us grownups get really tired and need extra sleep." she said, tickling him. They ate dinner and Cam chattered on about his day. Josh echoed him with gibberish we didn't understand. He wasn't really talking yet. After dinner Bethann cleaned up the kitchen and got the boys their baths. We were going to watch Monsters Inc. for a while before their bedtime.

"Baby, I need to step into the bedroom to make a call. I'll be out soon." I told her and kissed her before heading to our room to call Collum. She nodded and had the boys on either side of her with their stuffie's and blankets. I stood at the door looking at them for a few minutes. They were my family. I wasn't giving them up. Now to make sure they were safe. I closed the bedroom door and dialed my friend's number. It was his private line, nobody knew we were still in touch.

"O'Leary." Collum answered with his Irish brogue. "Whatcha calling me for, Seanie?" I grinned, he was the only one who called me that. "I haven't heard from ya in a long time."

"I'm sorry my old friend. Seems we have a mutual problem." I told him running my hand over my face. "I know you still use the local Rippers chapter there for muscle sometimes.

"Aye, but we don't discuss my business. You know that." Collum said curiously. I knew that it was against code for him to talk about the Family business with an outsider. "What is this mutual problem ye have, mate?"

"My father." I growled into the phone. "The bastard is planning to double cross you. The Sartori Family has a division in the ranks. Enzo has gone rogue. He is working with my father to kill his brother and make it look like the Irish did it."

"The fuck ya say?" Collum sounded pissed. "How did you find this out?"

"My woman's sister was involved with Enzo for a few years, she ran about eighteen months ago and took a stash of his cash he was holding to pay my father with. She came here to stay with her sister and have their second child. He didn't know about the second pregnancy. What he did notice was that his cash was missing. He found her and killed her before she could tell him where it was. We found it. We plan to give the money to Vincente tomorrow at a meeting to let him know what his brother had planned for him. We got a hold of two of Enzo's little minions and squeezed the information from them before finishing them off." I told him. I could almost hear the wheels turning in his head.

"Well, that changes things don't it." Collum sounded deadly calm. I wouldn't want to cross him. "I'll take care of your father. I think maybe it's about time for you and your brothers to do a cleaning of this chapter up here."

"Yep, I am planning to talk to Axle about that after we get this situation taken care of." I told him. "Wish I knew if there were any of them worth saving."

"I can look into that for ye. I have someone on the inside. He must not have known your pa's plan. I'll get back to you on the names. Meanwhile I'm going to take care of the traitor, Seamus 'Snake' McKay." Collum said and then disconnected the call. Damn, I wouldn't want to be in my father's shoes when Collum gets him. He is head of the Irish Family now for good reason. He is ruthless and mean. I put the phone in my pocket and went to join Bethann and the boys for the rest of the movie. I had already sent Fang a message that Gator would be covering for me tonight.

I walked over to the couch and Cameron held his arms out for me to pick him up. I scooped him up with his blanket and stuffie then sat down with him in my lap. Beth had Josh in her lap, and she laid her head on my shoulder while we watched the rest of the movie.

The next morning, we got up, had breakfast and headed over to the clubhouse. Lillian was already there, and Fury was watching her as usual. I wish he would just make a move. She has had plenty of time to mourn. It's time she moved on. I showed Bethann where she and the boys would be sleeping tonight. It would be late when we got back so we would just crash here. It was two rooms connected by a bathroom and she could keep the boys' side locked so they could only go to our room and bathroom. I placed their stuff inside and then we headed back to the common room. Bethann found a kid's channel for them to watch and put some toys down for them.

"I want to help. Let me go to the Diner. I know you won't let him hurt me." Bethann said looking up at me with those blue eyes. "You said he can't get in here so the boys would be safe too."

"Come on Hawk, you know we won't let anything happen to her. One of us will be at the back door and two watching the front. You will be there as well watching with your rifle." Blade said as he played with his favorite knife. I looked at him and looked at my girl. She was determined.

"Fuck, fine. But you will listen to whatever we tell you. If one of us says run, you run, duck, you duck. No arguments. Understood." I said, holding her closer to me.

"Yes Sir." She said in a breathy whisper and my cock decided to let me know how much he liked that.

"Damn." I mumbled under my breath, and she giggled. "Ok, we need to get going if we are doing this. I'm going to ride in the back seat lying down. She will drive her car and go into the diner. I need you guys in place before we get there so go."

"It will be fine. I trust you guys and I know you won't let him hurt me." She whispered to me. She grabbed a large purse to put the money in. I laid down on the floorboard of the backseat and she got in the front to drive us to the Diner. I fucking hate this plan. I really hope it works.

17

*B*ethann

I felt eyes on me as I walked into the Diner. I sat at a table in the middle of the room. I didn't want to be hidden in a booth. It was almost noon and I kept looking at the door. I ordered coffee just to have something to do with my hands. I had my purse in my lap. My wallet was still at the compound. The only thing in this purse was money and a tracker. They wanted him to be caught with it. I had a wire on me so they could hear and record our conversation. Actually, the wire was also in the purse. I was starting to wonder if he had figured it out when the door rang, and he walked inside. I would know him anywhere because my nephews looked just like him. He walked over to me and sat down.

"Ms. Todd, good of you to meet me. Now, we are going to sit here and have lunch then you are going to follow me to my car." He said smoothly looking at the menu.

"I'm not going anywhere with you. I have your money in my purse. You can take it and go away." I looked him in the eye and my blood ran cold.

"You will do as I say. I want my son back. He will be heir to my Family business one day. I know you have him. Your stupid sister would have made sure he was cared for. I would have given her another chance if she hadn't been parading her body around like a common whore. I couldn't have a stripper for my wife. At least you just managed the strip club. Now you will do as I say, or I will have to hurt you." Enzo sneered at me. "Get up and excuse yourself to the bathroom. You will go out the backdoor and I will meet you at my car."

"Fine, but don't hurt my nephew." I said as I got up to walk to the bathroom. I knew that the guys would grab him as soon as he got out the door. I went and locked myself in the bathroom. I pulled my phone from my back pocket and sent a text off to Hawk. He would let me know when it was safe to come out.

Taking a deep breath, I hopped on the counter to wait. Finally, I heard a knock on the bathroom door.

"Bethie, you can come out now." Hawk said. I jumped off the counter and unlocked the door. He pulled me into his arms and held me tight. "Never again. I thought I was going to lose my mind seeing him sitting within reaching distance of you."

"I'm fine, I'm guessing you got him." I said as he nodded. "Okay, then I need to get back to Cam and Josh. You guys have something to do."

"Yes, we do. Let's go." Hawk took my hand and led me to my car. He opened the passenger door and buckled me in then got on the driver's side and drove us to the clubhouse. "I would prefer you and the boys to stay here tonight. I'll come back here when it's done. We are not sure if it was just Enzo and his two bozos or if there was anyone else working directly with him here."

I was quiet on the way back. I hated that he had to go to Denver to meet the head of the Sartori Crime Family. I knew that he wanted to ensure they would not come after us. We pulled up to the clubhouse and I ran inside to see the boys. They were lying on the couch watching cartoons with Lillian. I could breathe again when I saw them. Hawk came up behind me and wrapped his arms around me.

"Baby, we will be back as soon as we can. I will have my phone on vibrate in my pocket. Text or call me if you need me. I'll let you know when I'm on my way home." He said as I turned around and he kissed me. "I love you. Stay here and stay safe for me."

"I love you too. Come home to us please." I said, watching him grab the bag of money and leave. I sat down in the armchair by the couch. Lillian looked over at me and reached out to take my hand and squeeze it, she knew how it felt to have to wait. I just prayed my situation turned out better.

"They will be fine. Those guys are tough as nails and smart as a whip." She said trying to reassure me. We played with the boys, fed them lunch. When they laid down for a nap, I laid down with them. I figured it would pass the time more quickly. I woke up and went into the living room to see the guys watching a football game. They glanced over at me and smiled.

"There are some hot wings, fried chicken and other snacks in the kitchen if you're hungry." Doc said. "We didn't want you girls to have to worry about dinner."

"Have you heard anything yet?" I asked hoping for some news. I bit my lip as they looked at me and shook their heads.

"It takes a couple of hours to get there. Then they have the meeting. We won't hear from them until it's over." Rider said gently. "You should eat something. Hawk will whoop my ass if I don't get you to eat."

"I'll try." I walked over and fixed a small plate with some hot wings, cheese cubes and a slice of pizza. I knew the boys would be hungry when they woke up. I sat down on the floor in front of the coffee table and ate while watching the game. I would take anything to distract me from the time. It felt like it was crawling so slow.

18

Hawk

The drive to Denver felt like the longest ever. We had Enzo's sorry ass knocked out in the truck. The money was in there with him. We were almost at the hotel for the meeting. My mind was all over the place. I wondered if Collum had found my father yet. I didn't need that asshole trying to come here and start shit. I knew he wouldn't act on the contract until he had his deposit. He was greedy like that. He would have already been setting the frame into motion. Collum promised to let me know when it was done.

We pulled into the parking garage and parked by the elevators. Axle checked to make sure Enzo was still knocked out and that he was secured. We didn't want him getting out or making a bunch of noise while we were inside meeting with his brother. Taking the elevator up to the restaurant we filed off and went to find Sartori. As we approached the large booth in the back a couple of his goons got up to meet us. It was standard procedure. We showed them what we were carrying and then shook hands with the boss.

"Gentleman, it is good of you to come. I appreciate that you have my back. Now what is it that you needed to tell me that we could not discuss over the phone." Vincente inquired with a raised eyebrow. The man was classically handsome and well dressed. Very polite, but we also knew his reputation. You did not cross him and expect to live.

"Sorry to bring you so far from home but we didn't feel comfortable coming to New York and Boston was out of the question. I'll get straight to the point, and we do have proof of what we are about to tell you." Axle said as he nodded to Fury and me.

"Okay, you have my attention." Vincente sat back crossing his arms over his chest.

"Your brother Enzo, he has been plotting to have you killed. He had money he had been hoarding to pay Seamus McKay to kill you and then frame the Irish for the job. His girlfriend, whom he had been abusing for years, found his stash and took it to get away from him. He finally found her, and he killed her leaving her son an orphan. Thankfully her sister is happy to raise him as her own." I told him gaging his reactions. The man would be an excellent poker player because he never changed his expression.

"You say you have proof of my brother's disloyalty? I'd like to see that." Vincente said as Fury moved to show him the video, he took of the confessions he got out of the two goons.

"Do you recognize those two men in the pictures?" Axle asked him. "They were following his woman around snapping pictures and making threats."

"Yes, those are the Balducci cousins. They always follow my brother around like puppies." He smirked as he looked up at Fury. "I assume by the videos and photos that they are dead."

"You assume correctly. We don't take well to people threatening our women." I told him with a scowl on my face.

"I see, and the money they were looking for. I assume that you have it with you?" he asked as he looked at us.

"We do, along with your brother in the trunk of our car. He is still alive. We figured you would prefer to deal with him personally. We know how you hate a traitor. Blood or not." Axle said with a smirk of his own. "The money is in the trunk with him. We need to make the exchange somewhere there are no cameras."

"If you will follow us to the private airfield, we can take custody of him there. What is it that you want in return?" Vincente inquired.

"We want your promise that you will leave your nephew and his aunt alone. Allow us to raise the boy as ours." I said firmly. "You will have heirs of your own to pass your business to. We want to raise Bethann's nephew as ours. He has been through enough losing his mother to a senseless crime."

"Agreed, I have no need for my nephew to be raised in the business. Before I kill Enzo, I will have papers drawn up signing over his parental rights to her. I'll have them overnighted to you." Vincente stood up. "What about the other traitor?"

"The O'Leary's will handle him. It's a blood debt. McKay is my father, we are also Irish by birth. They consider it a huge betrayal and will end him painfully." I said as I looked him in the eye. "I have no love for the man. He was a bastard when I was growing up and that has not changed."

"Understood, let's go finish this shall we?" Vincente laid down some money on the table for their drinks and we followed them to the airstrip.

When we arrived, he motioned for his guys to follow him to the trunk. We opened it up and pulled Enzo out. He was awake. When he saw his brother, his eyes widened. I handed Vincente the bag with the money in it.

"It's probably missing some due to Candy needing living expenses but everything that was there when she died is in that bag. I'd say close to a quarter of a million dollars." I told him as he handed the bag to one of his men. He walked over to his brother and whispered something to him. Enzo whimpered and started to shake.

"Get this traitor on the plane. When we get home take him to my warehouse and chain him up. We will deal with him first thing tomorrow. He can have the rest of the night to contemplate what will happen to him." Vincente said watching the men take his brother to the plane. "Thank you again." He shook our hands and then left. We watched as the plane took off and then got back into the car to head home.

"Well now you can rest easy." Fury said as we were driving back towards Liberty. "You don't have to worry about them coming after the boys."

"I won't rest easy until I know Collum has my father in his custody. He is a mean bastard and if he finds out that I warned the O'Leary's he will be out for blood." I said as I sent my girl a text to let her know we were on our way home.

Bethann: **We are fine, just finished eating dinner and watching football with the guys. The boys ate, played a while and went back to bed. See you when you get home. Love you.**

Hawk: **Love you too, keep the bed warm for me. Be naked when I get there.**

"I know that look. Someone is getting laid when he gets home." Fury chuckled. Hawk whacked him on the back of the head. Axle laughed out loud.

"You deserve to be happy Hawk, and we all like Bethann." Axle said. The rest of the drive home was quiet.

19

Bethann

I smiled at his message and put my phone on the end table beside me. Lillian looked over at me, her eyes questioning. I winked at her and nodded.

"They are on the way home. Everything went fine." I told her and noticed the relief. I think she was concerned about Fury, although she would never admit it. We had settled in to wait, watching the rest of the last football game with the guys.

Lillian got up and announced that she was going to bed, and she would sleep in the room with my nephews so that Hawk and I could have time undisturbed when he got back. I think she wanted to avoid seeing Fury, but I wasn't going to call her out for it.

I headed off to get ready for bed myself and slipped naked under the covers to wait for my guy. I must have fallen asleep because I woke up to the feeling of whiskers sliding along my neck and him kissing down my chest. I stretched and put my hands on his head holding him to me. Mmm, what a way to wake up. I opened my eyes and stared into the most beautiful green eyes I had ever seen in the face of the man I loved with my whole heart. I bit my lip as he resumed his journey down my body. Licking and sucking my skin into his mouth making sure to leave his marks all over me. By the time he got to my core I knew I was soaked. He took a deep breath and moaned as he licked through my folds and started to feast on me. I was writhing and panting with need. It felt amazing and he slipped a finger inside me then two working them around and pumping in and out while he continued to flick my clit with the tip of his tongue. Suddenly I felt a wet digit breach my back hole and I came all over his face. My legs were twitching, and I could feel my pussy pulsing with my orgasm. He looked up at me licking his lips and then climbed up my body thrusting inside me. I held on to his shoulders as he fucked me hard and fast. I bit into his shoulder and sucked him marking him as well. He reached down and grabbed my ass to hold me closer and pound me harder until I went over the edge again taking him with me. He eased down laying his head on my chest and I ran my hands over his back. I didn't want to move. I loved his weight on me. Suddenly he got up and I heard the water running. He came back with a washcloth to clean me up. Then crawled back into bed and fell asleep holding me close.

The next morning, we got up and gathered the boys to head back to the house. It had started snowing on their way home last night and now the ground was covered. We decided to bundle them up and play in the snow. We made snowmen and snow angels, then we had a snowball fight and Josh couldn't stop laughing. Cameron was laughing and throwing snowballs at me. He had taken Hawk's side. We played until I knew they were hungry and tired. Taking them inside we gave them a bath and put on dry clothes. I fixed them a grilled cheese sandwich and a cut up banana on the side for lunch then they went down for a nap.

We had changed into warm clothes as well. Hawk started a fire in the fireplace, and we curled up on the couch with a blanket and some hot cocoa. Rider had gone to the grocery store for us and packed the pantry with things so we would not have to leave all weekend. It was wonderful. I knew he was still worried about his father and that the guys were talking about having to shut down the Boston chapter. They wanted to try to salvage anyone they could but some of them would just have to be put down. They were vicious and crooked as hell.

"What are you thinking about baby?" he asked me as he rubbed my back. I snuggled into him and sighed.

"I'm just thinking that I have never been this happy before. I'm wondering where we go from here." I said wondering if we would be staying in his house or if we needed to move and would date.

"I was hoping that you and the boys would stay here with me. I love you all and want to be a husband to you and a father to them." He sat up and looked at me. Reaching over he pulled a ring box from his jacket pocket. He opened it and there was a round diamond on a beautiful gold band. I looked up at him and he had tears in his eyes.

"I love you so much. You and those boys are my whole world. Please say you will marry me, and we can adopt them." He asked me. I was so choked up I couldn't speak so I just nodded and threw my arms around him. "I'm going to assume that is a yes."

"Yes, a thousand times, yes!" I said as I rained kisses all over his handsome face. "How will we do that?" I told her what Vincente said and that we would be getting the papers tomorrow.

"Do you think you would want more kids baby?" he asked me hesitantly. "I'd love to add one to the mix. Maybe a little girl with your beautiful hair."

"I'd love that. I hope she has your eyes." I whispered and kissed him again. "You didn't use any protection last night when you got home. So, it is a real possibility."

"Good. How soon can we get married?" he asked me. "I don't want to wait. I'm ready for you to be mine forever."

"I'm already yours but I would like a small ceremony here with our friends and family." I told him and the smile on his face just melted me.

"Done, I'll get Annie, Sophie and Lillian working on it. How about two weeks from tomorrow?" he suggested.

"I love it." I told him and looked up to see Cameron come into the living room. He came over and climbed into Hawk's lap.

"Are you gonna be my Daddy and Auntie Beth my mommy, cause our mommy went to heaven and we needs a new one." He asked. I didn't know how to respond to that.

"How about if you call her Mama and leave Mommy for the one who went to heaven. You get to have two moms and I would love to be your Daddy." Hawk said as he hugged Cameron. Josh hollered out so I went to get him. He pointed to Hawk and said "Da".

My man about melted on the spot. He hugged the boys and smiled at me so big. It was the best day ever. We spent the weekend holed up playing with the boys and watching Disney movies. I had to go back to work Monday and Hawk would be back to splitting nights at the club. Hopefully they could hire a fulltime manager soon and a new bouncer so my man could do something else with his time. I just felt like I was waiting for the other shoe to drop.

20

Hawk

We had been back to business as usual for about a week. Lillian came over to keep the kids and Bethann went back to work. I was still waiting to hear from Collum about my father. It made me nervous that I had not heard anything yet. There was a reason he was given the name Snake. He was slippery and vicious. Striking without warning. I was interviewing for some new help at Trixie's. I just had no interest in being there anymore. Fang was more into painting bikes and was just filling in until we could be replaced. I had to work tonight so I was going to make a call to Collum and see if he had found him yet. Suddenly my phone went off and I saw it was Axle calling.

"Yeah man, what's up?" I asked him when I answered. I could feel that something was wrong.

"I need you at the clubhouse as quickly as possible. We have a problem." He said and hung up. Well damn, I knew things had been too quiet. I headed over to the clubhouse and went straight to the long table where we had our meetings. Everyone was there except for Fury.

I looked around not seeing him anywhere and then saw the looks on the guys' faces.

"Where is Fury?" I asked, starting to not like the vibe I was getting. Undertaker pointed at the box on the table. I had a sick feeling. I remembered what happened to Bear and Valkryie's father. I had just been a prospect and the box was given to me. I walked over and looked inside. When I saw there was no head, I let out the breath I was holding. Inside was his cut and a note.

You took something of mine so now I have something of yours. You owe me 250K if you want to see your brother again. Hawk knows where to find me.

Snake

"Son of a bitch, I'll fucking kill him myself." I said as I kicked a chair and felt my head pound. "I want to know how the hell they got him. Fury is no pussy, and he would not have been easy to take."

"Call your Irish friend. We are going to need help. Seems some of us are making a trip up to Boston." Axle said as he went to put Fury's cut in his office. "Looks like we will be shutting down that chapter sooner than we planned."

"Damn right. I have some calls to make." I stomped out of the clubhouse and headed to town. The first call was to Collum.

"O'Leary speaking." Collum answered. "Seannie, I know why your callin` and I was about to call you. We found your father, I took great pleasure in killing the bastard. He was working over one of your guys. We managed to save him, but he is in bad shape. I figured your people would want to take care of him so we put him on a plane, and it will be landing at the private airstrip outside of Denver in a few hours. I'm sorry we didn't get him sooner. You should bring a van, he will be on a hospital bed."

"Fuck, thank you for saving my friend. We will be sending someone to close down the Boston chapter soon." I told him. I heard him sigh and knew it wasn't good. "What have you not told me Collum?"

"There'll be no need to send anyone as there isn't anything left of them. It's done." He said and disconnected the call. I put the phone back in my pocket and headed back to the clubhouse to break the news and to get Doc to get his Medical Van.

I told them what happened, and we went to collect our brother from the airstrip. Doc rode in the back with him to make sure he stayed sedated and comfortable. We would take him home and nurse him back to health. Damn shame he wouldn't have anyone to get revenge on after he is better. They took him to Doc's place for now since he had a couple of rooms made up for patients that needed round-the-clock care. It didn't happen often but on occasion it did.

I decided to wait until Bethann got home to tell her what happened. She told me she wanted to go to the courthouse and get married today. We could have a ceremony when Fury was well enough to be there for it. So that's what we did. Lillian stood as our witness along with Rider.

Bethann made a beautiful bride even though she was just wearing a pants suit and some heels. She said they would wait until spring for their ceremony/party. We left the boys with Undertaker and Annie so we could take a short honeymoon. We were blessed to have each other, and we were going to celebrate each day as it came. Our friend was still alive, and our enemies were not, so that was a win.

The End

Made in United States
Troutdale, OR
05/17/2024

19937031R00060